KIERA

Dear Maggie,
You are loved!
~ Kate Willis

KIERA

KATE WILLIS

For Mikayla, Kaitlyn, Es, Nechet,
and everyone else who has been a "Destiny" to me.
I am blessed to have your friendship!

And for my Savior, Who has loved me with an everlasting love.

Scripture taken from the New King James Version®. Copyright
© 1982 by Thomas Nelson. Used by permission. All rights
reserved.

Cover design by PerryElisabethDesign.com with images from
DepositPhotos.com
Editing by KelseyBryantAuthor.weebly.com

Published by Toward Home Press

Printed in the United States of America
ISBN-13: 978-1721009886 ISBN-10: 1721009884

Website: OnceUponAnOrdinary.wordpress.com

Contents

Gathering Storms 9

No Place to Hide 19

Worry 29

Wishes 37

In the World 45

Anchor 57

Decisions 65

Gold 79

Settling In 85

Church 93

Mommy 101

Gray Fabric 109

Easter Sunday 119

Not of the World 131

Prayer 143

A Faithful Few 151

Flicker 163

Hosting Church 175

Thorne 185

Paperwork 201

Heightened Security 211

Babysitting 223

Shadow Puppets 233

The Trial 239

Brennan 249

Rain 251

Sparrows 263

Acknowledgments 281

About the Author 283

Also By This Author… 284

CHAPTER ONE
Gathering Storms

The earth felt cool against her skin as she ran her fingers through the rich, black soil and pulled up a hardy weed that blocked the sunlight from her plants. She smiled at the tiny lettuce sprout she had freed and wiped her hands on her oversized sweatshirt.

"There you go. Now you can breathe," she said, grinning at the long row of little leaves. They were the first plants to come up, but with a little sun and a lot of love, others would follow.

The breeze spun her light-brown hair in messy waves around her shoulders as she moved toward the other raised garden bed. Her flower garden. The soil was flat, undisturbed by any traces of green.

"Soon enough," she told herself. Warm anticipation filled her, but she shivered the next moment.

A gust of wind blew across the yard, and the new leaves of the shade trees danced furiously. The young woman brushed her hair back from her face and glanced up, shading her eyes against the retreating sun. Gray clouds stretched across the sky and vied for a place on the horizon.

She sprinted across the soft, synthetic grass to the covered porch and pulled open the glass door. She slid into a chair at the kitchen desk and waved her hand at the device screen.

The kitchen faucet was turned off for a moment. "Back so soon, honey?"

"I think there's a storm, Mom."

"What kind?"

She didn't answer as she paged through the apps, looking for the weather one. They were always being reordered on the family device.

"Kiera, what kind?" Mom came over with a wrinkled carrot in one hand and a peeler in the other. A crease showed above her glasses.

"Radiation," Kiera sighed. "Really high levels." She gestured to the map of their neighborhood with the pulsing, animated circle of storm front.

Mom pursed her lips. "Oh, dear. I suppose dinner will be indoors tonight then. No barbecue, so I'll have to think of another main dish."

"I'm sure Thorne won't mind," Kiera said with a smile that brought an answering one to her mom's face.

Mom disappeared into the pantry and came out a moment later with several jars of spaghetti sauce. "It's a blessing he is able to get the time off. And Pastor Silas will enjoy leading the Bible study again, even if it is just this once."

Another gust of wind blew against the house, and Kiera sprang up from the chair, leaving it swiveling behind her as she dashed outside.

Keeping one eye on the lightning-torn sky, she hauled both raised garden beds under the porch cover and pulled the waterproof shades down. She hooked them securely in place and checked them twice. She didn't want to risk letting her garden get rained on. That would mean starting over.

"Jade eats meatballs, right?" Mom asked when she entered the kitchen again.

Kiera grimaced and shrugged apologetically. "I'm not sure what she eats right now. Hunger strike can rear its ugly head at any time."

"If you can make it past her being two years old, I promise babysitting might be easy again," Mom encouraged.

Kiera grinned. "I just hope it doesn't ruin Thorne's family time too much to share his evening."

Mom looked at her over her glasses, eyebrows raised.

Kiera giggled. "Thorne is probably the last one to mind her, isn't he? I don't think he'd ever forgive me if I canceled her coming over the one night he was home."

"There would definitely be trouble. Your brother

loves that tiny girl like you wouldn't believe!"

"I can't think of anyone who doesn't, but he wins the prize for her most devoted admirer." Kiera peeked over her mom's shoulder at the beginnings of dinner. "Anything I can help with?"

"If you roll these meatballs, I'll take care of salad assembly," Mom said, flicking her curly hair back over her shoulders.

Kiera flopped her sweatshirt over the desk chair and rinsed the hardened dirt off her fingers. She searched through the apps again to look for the meatball recipe. Where was the document app? It should have been near the top since she used it every day for school.

Thunder crashed outside and her hand slipped to an app she never used. News. And the worst news she could ever imagine staring her in the face.

"Mom?" Her voice swayed like the shade trees.

"What is it, Kiera?"

"I know you told me to never look at the news app, but this was an accident. I saw the newest headline." She was crying now, not with her eyes but with her voice. "We lost a devastating number of soldiers, and the president is calling for a draft."

Somewhere behind her, Mom dropped a dish. Lightning flashed through the blinds in front of her, lighting up her face and the tears shining in her eyes. A storm of another kind was coming.

Kiera hurried up the stairs and shut her bedroom door behind her. Crossing over to her window, she pulled back the curtain. Rain streaked her window, and lightning angled across the sky in a fierce storm. A raindrop rolled down the window, and she traced its path with her finger. So many tears.

She pulled back from the window. There was just enough time to touch up her makeup and change into nicer clothes before Dad and Thorne arrived. Grabbing a cozy maroon sweater and a clean skirt, she changed quickly and forced her mind to think of other things.

The salad was waiting in a cut glass bowl at the very center of the table. The places were set. The squash spaghetti and meatballs were being kept warm on the stove ready to be served. Everything was just perfect. Everything but the news that had blasted through the device screen into their peaceful kitchen. She squeezed her thumb and shut her eyes.

Fear rose up inside her stomach again, crowding out her hunger for dinner. She hurried over to her desk and glanced in the mirror, momentarily ignoring the Bible reading reminder she had posted for herself. Her brown eyes had a smeared shadow of mascara under them from the tears she couldn't hold back.

"Just focus on the good evening you are going to have. Don't think about the draft. Don't think about being almost eighteen. And don't think about what happened to Shannon Stewart," she told her reflection fiercely. Another tear leaked out of her narrowed eyes.

Running a brush through her windswept hair, she pulled it back from her face and pinned it in a messy bun. The cool cloth she rubbed over her cheeks removed her makeup and a little of the feverish heat from too many tears. She reapplied mascara and the last of her lipstick. It was time to make cosmetics again. Destiny had promised to do it with her when she came over next time.

The doorbell jerked her from her planning, and she hurried downstairs to greet whoever had arrived first. It was Daddy, and both she and Mom were more than glad to see him. He pulled Kiera into a tight hug; and she felt all the nervousness, fear, and questions melt away. He would protect her in every way possible.

While Mom carried him away to discuss the day's events, Kiera drifted into the kitchen and stirred the spaghetti sauce again. Checked the temperature of the meatballs. Filled the glasses with water to exactly the same height. Made brave faces at her reflection in the side of the pot.

She was stirring the sauce for the third time when the doorbell finally rang again. She propped the spoon against the pot and ran to answer it. Thorne this time. He leaned his dripping umbrella against the side of the house and came in.

"Heya, Kiera!" Thorne grinned at her as he gave her a quick hug.

"Heya, Thorne!" She led him into the kitchen. "I'm so glad you could come. We even made your favorite—squash spaghetti."

"I could've guessed. The whole street smells good from it," Thorne replied, his brown eyes smiling as he took the glass of water she offered him. "And what heavenly part of this meal was your contribution?"

"Well, you horrific flatterer, I rolled meatballs, picked salad vegetables, and set the table, but everything else was Mom's doing. Oh, and I made the ice cream. You might get some."

"What did I do to deserve this?"

"Nothing. It's all grace, Pastor," she teased. "Oh, and we just remembered that we get Jade tonight. Do you mind?"

He took a big swallow of water. "Mind Jade? Brain check." He tapped his temple.

Kiera grinned. "That's an old joke. If I go to the hospital tonight, it will definitely be from all this grinning."

"I'm delighted Jade's coming," Thorne said. "This place needs livening up; you're getting too old." He gave her an innocent face over his glass as he drained it.

Kiera shook her head in amusement. "What would I do without my oldest brother?"

"Miss your annual birthday chocolate, maybe?" He winked and pulled a small, flat package out of his jeans pocket.

"Okay, you're my hero, and I forgive you for everything, I think." The doorbell interrupted before she could take it.

Kiera opened the door and smiled widely at the tiny girl standing there. "Jade! I'm so happy to see you!" She picked her up and gave her a squeeze. "Did you bring dollies?"

"Um... Daddy hash dollies," Jade explained around her thumb.

"Dollies and a lot more," her daddy said, coming inside and sliding the diaper bag strap off his shoulder in relief.

"Thank you for bringing them, Brennan," Kiera said from behind the toddler's curly head. "She's been wanting me to meet them."

"Poor Brennan's gonna break his shoulder someday, though," Thorne said, eyeing the heavy diaper bag.

Brennan smiled wryly and ran his fingers through his wild dark hair. "How are you, Pastor Thorne?"

"Grateful to spend time with some of my family tonight." Thorne reached out to shake his friend's hand. "How are you?"

"I'm all right."

"I think you all are in for a big treat with Pastor Silas leading the Bible study. He told me the Lord has been laying a lot on his heart lately. I hate to miss it, but I'm glad for the break. Between some difficult leadership meetings, several Easter sermons to prepare, and that wedding in a few weeks, life is full."

"Well, you're in my prayers every day," Brennan said earnestly. "I'd love to stay and talk more, but Bible study is starting in just a few, and the cars are slower from the rain."

"All right. Get out of here and have a blessed time." Thorne slapped him on the back.

Brennan grinned and turned away. "Kiera, I remembered her blanket this week, so hopefully it won't be so disastrous when she gets tired." He grimaced.

"It's all right, but thanks all the same," Kiera said with a laugh.

"Thanks for watching her."

"You're welcome." She shut the door behind him as he went outside into the rain. Jade wriggled in her arms, and she set her down, tweaking one of the toddler's tiny braids. She must have spent the morning at the Whites'. Mrs. White always braided Jade's hair.

"You're doing Brennan and his daughter a great service, you know," Thorne said, leaning down and tickling Jade. She giggled and squirmed away to hide behind Kiera's skirt.

"Thank you. I've gotten quite attached to my little friend." She looked behind her and smiled at Jade. "Have you said hello to Mom and Dad yet?"

"No, I haven't, come to think of it. Have you seen them around?"

"Dining room, maybe?" Kiera picked up the heavy

diaper bag and took Jade's hand. "We're gonna go play dollies."

CHAPTER TWO
No Place to Hide

Kiera pulled an old T-shirt over Jade's pink-striped dress and buckled her into the highchair. Dad and Mom took their places across the table from each other, and Thorne sat down in the remaining chair.

"This dinner looks amazing," Thorne said, surveying the dining table. "Thanks for preparing it, Mom and Kiera."

"You're welcome, son," Mom said.

"I hope Jade thinks as highly of it as you do," Kiera said, half-dreading what was coming.

"If you need to feed her something else, there are leftovers in the refrigerator," Mom offered, straightening the lace table runner.

"Thanks for the offer, but I think I'll try this first. That's how we made it through 'food strike' last time," Kiera replied, cutting a single meatball into tiny pieces. She separated three squash "noodles" and one leaf of lettuce onto Jade's plate.

"Wise girl. Shall we pray?" Dad said, taking Mom's hand and reaching for Kiera's. Thorne slid his device into his pocket. "Dear Father, thank you for this food and family time. Please give us Your guidance and protection in the days ahead. In Your name, amen."

Kiera opened her eyes after the "amen" and directed a smile at Jade. "It's time to eat now."

"No," Jade muttered and shook her head, her braids swinging back and forth over her shoulders.

"Here, try some."

The toddler's whole face sagged into a pout, and she turned away. Kiera chased her mouth with a noodle and slipped it in.

Out came the noodle, which was quickly replaced by a piece of meatball. Jade swallowed it and turned to hide her face in the highchair.

Kiera caught a snatch of the conversation.

"If one or both of them is drafted, they are going to need help with the children," Thorne was saying.

She knew they were talking about her brother Jordan and his wife, Niyanna. She wasn't the only one whose life would be drastically changed by the draft.

"Jade, look at me. You need to eat some salad too," Kiera said.

"No, no. No." Jade opened her mouth to protest and in went a small leaf.

Jade slammed herself against the back of her highchair and kicked her legs at the offensive green vegetable. Angry tears mixed with the sauce on her face.

"Do you mind if I take her to the kitchen?" Kiera directed this question mostly to her brother.

"Go ahead, if you think that's what is needed," Thorne replied with an encouraging wink.

Dad nodded and Mom moved to help her carry both plates into the kitchen.

"Thanks a billion," she replied, scooting the highchair along behind Mom.

Mom closed the device and set both plates down on the desk. Then she laid a gentle hand on her daughter's shoulder. "Kiera, don't forget to pray for patience."

Kiera let out a sigh and nodded. "Thanks."

Mom left the kitchen, and Kiera walked over to the sink to rinse her hands, buying herself a little time. She could hear the conversation in the dining room slowly begin again, though their voices were low, almost as if they didn't want her to listen.

"They're pretty desperate for soldiers." Thorne's voice was flat. "Recalling veterans; offering first-time mothers abortions or embryo storage. No wonder there are no exemptions for Kiera."

"It's too late to leave the country even." Mom's voice. Kiera dried her hands on a towel, but her cheeks were wet with tears.

Dad sounded more tired than she had ever heard him. "Our only hope is that she will somehow fail the physical examination, but that would take a miracle."

Kiera sucked in a shuddering breath and turned away to Jade, determined to focus on the need at hand. Saying a quick prayer before sitting down in the desk chair, she rolled the highchair up directly in front of her. Making sure the blinds were down, she settled into a battle that would most likely include some correction. Brennan had allowed her to use it when necessary. Tonight might be one of those times.

Half an hour and several noodles later, Kiera entered the dining room with Jade perched on her hip.

"We return victorious in time for ice cream!" Kiera announced with a relieved smile.

Jade clapped her hands together. "Yay, ice cream!"

Kiera sat on the living room floor with her back against the couch and her legs stretched out in front of her. Her fingers typed furiously away on the journaling app. She had a long and fruitful day behind her to tell about, but this would have to be a quick update.

The sound of laughter made her look up to see Dad and Thorne scrambling to pick up the playing cards that had spilled under the coffee table. Mom's eyes sparkled with mischief, and she winked at Kiera across the room like Thorne always did. Kiera made a goofy face in reply.

Turning her head slightly to check on Jade sleeping on the couch behind her, she saw Thorne coming over to sit with her.

"Competition too fierce for you?" she teased, brushing a dust bunny out of his hair.

He laughed and the lines next to his eyes showed deeper for a moment. "I'm ready for a little break. What are you doing?" he asked quietly, peering over her shoulder at the half-written entry.

"Nothing that can't wait a little while I talk to my favorite oldest brother," she said, setting the device down next to her. "I'm really sorry I missed most of dinner with everyone."

"That little girl," Thorne replied, twisting around to look at the sleeping toddler, "is much more important than my evening. Training little ones isn't a distraction from more important work, it *is* the most important work."

"Thanks."

"I stole that from C. S. Lewis, of course. Pastor Thorne paraphrase."

She laughed. "Brennan says Jade's usually good about eating at home, but I guess she's just starting a new phase. Think I should warn him?"

"Nah." Thorne shook his head and winked.

Kiera bit back a conspiratorial smile.

"I'd like to try again on giving you that birthday chocolate," Thorne said, taking the package out of his pocket again.

"Oh, thank you! Oo, Mandie's? That's the best." She peeled back the wrapping and broke off a square, letting the rich goodness melt on her tongue.

"Heavenly. Do you want some?"

Thorne shook his head. "No, thanks. I'm too full of maple ice cream."

Kiera smiled and yawned. "What are you preaching about on Sunday?"

"Being in the world but not of it." He shrugged at the grimace she gave him. "That's just where I happen to be in the text, and no matter what I say, they won't agree with it. They have conservative, agreeable Sunday faces, but I can tell when my words are met with hostility." He sighed, then winked at her. "But I talk with the Lord, and He reminds me His sheep still need to be fed whether or not they belong to Him just yet. So I keep sharing the truth."

"That's a good way to think of it, 'Jeremiah'."

Thorne smiled again.

"And how's Pastor Silas been? We were surprised he was able to lead the Bible study tonight." Kiera hugged her knees to herself and played with the tip of one toe that peeked through her sock. She loved these quiet conversations with her oldest brother.

"I was surprised when he offered. He's been down a lot these past few weeks, but he seems to be doing better lately." Thorne wiped his forehead with the back of his hand. "Jessica keeps me updated in our meetings about the pro-life ministry."

"Jessica, eh?" Kiera looked sideways at him.

"Yup. Jessica." His face went impossibly blank. "Did you decide if you were coming to the rally?"

"I'm hoping to catch a ride with the Moores, but I don't know if Mom and Dad are coming yet. I'm looking forward to it though," she said, grinning.

"Me too." He stretched and pulled himself to his feet. "I don't get to see you all nearly often enough. But after those Easter sermons and the wedding, I'll have a little more time."

"Do you have your suit picked out yet, Pastor?" Kiera asked.

"Yep. Just a little more premarital counseling with the couple, and they'll be ready too." Thorne yawned. "I wasn't sure about them at first, but Shelby's a nice girl. I have a feeling she'll pull him closer to God."

"Maybe so."

"Hey, I wanted to tell you that Dad, Mom, and I talked about the draft a bit this evening."

Kiera stiffened and answered slowly, "I guessed that from what I could hear." This was something she didn't want to think about again. She stood up to face him. "And?"

He placed an affectionate hand on her arm. "I just wanted to let you know that God and I are on the job."

"Thanks a billion."

"Goodnight, Kiera," he said, giving her a quick hug.

"Goodnight, brother."

Dad and Mom took a break from their game to say goodbye, help him find his shoes, and send him home with a heaping plate of leftovers, but she hardly took any notice of them or Jade's peaceful breathing behind her. She stared at the opposite wall, trying to calm herself down enough to stop shaking. She squeezed her thumb with all four fingers, then released it.

There was no hiding from the draft. Everyone was in the government's system since the day they were born. But a draft now? After so many years of peace, it was a nightmare no one had even imagined.

She began to pray, pouring out her fears and her mustard seed faith before God. Giving it all to Him to do with as He pleased.

A light knock sounded on the front door, and she got up to answer it, grateful for the distraction. She was still shaking when she greeted Brennan, but she forced herself to smile and say quietly, "She's asleep on the couch."

Brennan smiled and followed her into the living room. "Hey, Princess," he said in low tones and gathered the tiny girl up in his arms.

Kiera handed him the repacked diaper bag, and he slid the strap expertly over his shoulder as he moved toward the door.

"How did she do?"

"All right. We had a bit of a struggle over dinner, and I had to use some correction; but we had fun with her dolls," Kiera replied, sliding the little girl's shoes on slowly so she wouldn't wake her.

"Your birthday is this Saturday, right?"

"Yes." She was surprised he remembered.

"I was thinking I could keep Jade so—"

"Oh. No." She looked up at him and cut him off, guessing what he was about to say. "I want to babysit her. It will just be us and Destiny and her family. Jade won't be any trouble at all."

"You're sure?" He lifted his eyebrows in question.

She nodded and swallowed, holding back sudden tears.

"Are you okay?" Brennan looked at her with concern and shifted Jade in his arms.

"Yeah, no. I'm fine." She gestured with her hand as if brushing the emotions away.

Brennan watched her closely for a moment, not quite satisfied with her answer.

Kiera smiled. "See you guys Saturday."

"All right then. Thanks again."

Thorne was finally leaving just when Brennan was, and he walked out with him to discuss the Bible study. Kiera shut the door behind them, then pressed her forehead against the cool, hard boards. Getting drafted would mean leaving her family. Leaving Jade.

Please, God. Do something.

She turned away and hurried upstairs before anyone could ask her what was the matter. She definitely didn't feel like explaining right now.

CHAPTER THREE
Worry

Kiera glanced up through the open blinds at the afternoon traffic snaking past the kitchen window. She pulled up the note app and typed something into it, then brought her screen and mental focus back to the task at hand. An essay was due that evening, and she still had half a dog-eared page of odd scientific phrases, measurements, and her own random observations to combine into something readable.

"Wow, I have no idea what that word means," she commented loudly over the music in her earbuds.

Typing the troublesome word into the question app, she read a short article and returned to her essay with new understanding. A notification popped up, but she shut it quickly. Time enough to view it later.

When she had exhausted her notes, she leaned back in her chair and scrutinized the essay for correct grammar and punctuation. Mom came to stand behind her chair, and she paused the music and pulled out her earbuds.

"No sneak peeks," she teased, covering the device screen with both hands.

"Don't worry. I won't grade it until you're ready," Mom replied, smiling.

"Oh, good! If you went off this version, I think I'd definitely flunk science," Kiera said.

"Sorry for the interruption, but I had a quick question. The storm is wearing off, so we should be able to go outside tomorrow. Do you want to work that into your birthday plans?"

Kiera's stomach clenched at the mention of her birthday, but she pushed the feeling away. "Destiny and I will be mostly indoors with the cosmetic making, but I'm sure her brothers will be glad for the chance to escape 'Girldom', as they call it."

Mom laughed and shook her head. "Those boys!"

"But hey, if we still have the ingredients for the barbecue you were talking about yesterday, we could eat outside."

"That sounds like a good idea."

"Thanks so much for helping to make my birthday as wonderful as possible," Kiera said, spinning her chair around to face her mom.

Tears sprang into her eyes, and Mom pulled her into a hug. "It's going to be all right. I promise. Whatever happens, God will work it out in the end."

Kiera buried her face in Mom's comforting shoulder for a moment and rested in the safety she could always find there. Her mom was speaking the truth, but often actions meant more than spoken words.

"Thanks, Mom," Kiera whispered.

"Any time. I'll let you get back to your paper right now while I go spelunking in the refrigerator. 'Those boys' do eat a lot more than your Jade."

Kiera was still smiling as she replaced her earbuds and returned to fussing with her paper. She clicked out of the document app the moment she was done and allowed herself to read her long-awaited messages.

There was one from Destiny and another from Brennan Stewart. She opened Destiny's first.

> Hey, you!!!
> How be thee? I am soooo excited about tomorrow!!!! <3 (The boys are too, though they won't admit it. Probably just for the ice cream reason, but who knows.) I'm bringing extra beet powder since my colors are darker than yours, and I don't want to use all of your stuff up. Anything else I should bring?
> Fist bumps and firecrackers, Destiny

Kiera laughed. "Mom, you have to see this."

Mom adjusted her glasses and scanned over the message. "Tell her to bring her enthusiasm, and we don't need anything else." Her smile was wide.

Kiera hurried to respond.

Hey, girly!

This message probably single-handedly made my day. (Although it will be competing soon if I pass science. Pray!) Just bring your enthusiasm, that beet powder, and something to prank your brothers with; and we'll be good. ;P

Fist bumps and firecrackers, Kiera

"What did Brennan say?" Mom asked as Kiera closed the device.

"Oops, I almost forgot to read that. I bet it's about babysitting. Bad me. Let's see…" She reopened the app and scrolled through the long stream of promotions to find his message. "He says, 'Kiera, I was thinking I could bring Jade by early in the morning and pick her up after lunch. How does that sound to you?'"

Mom snorted in amusement. "He needs to take lessons from Destiny."

"Or Kent even," Kiera added. She typed back.

If you're worried about cutting into the party, don't think that at all. We're fine. She is a party. I'll take her as long as you need.

Blessings, Kiera Clark

"Good morning, Daddy!" Kiera said, hugging him. Saturdays were her favorite since he was home to share it with her and Mom.

"Good morning, little sparrow," Dad replied,

hugging her back. His salt-and-pepper hair was carefully combed even though it wasn't a workday. "And happy birthday!"

"Thanks, Dad," she answered, smile wavering slightly.

"Let tomorrow worry about itself and focus on the blessings of today. How about it?" Dad tweaked the end of her nose.

She grinned bravely in reply. "I'll try it," she said, but while he was busy preparing himself a cup of coffee, she slipped upstairs to calm her soul before her Savior.

It was something she had neglected for a few days. Birthday preparations and final school tests were distracting. She couldn't remember the last time she had paused for a long talk with her Lord. Now she had time to think, the aching, fearful gap between her and God was larger than she had guessed. She hadn't even thought to finish the prayer time she was attempting when Brennan interrupted her two days before.

Locking her bedroom door and curling up on the floor, she told God everything. She thanked Him for her hilarious, loving, big family, for Jade, for her plants, for the books Brennan loaned her, for Destiny's coming over. For eighteen years of life, for chocolate frosting, for everything she could think of.

She told Him she was sorry for not talking to Him enough or reading His Word as often as she should. She asked for help conquering her fear of the draft and keeping her heart straight about relating to young men. She asked for strength to focus on today only and guidance for the days to come.

Feeling much more refreshed, Kiera stood up and stretched. There was probably a really complicated carpet imprint on her face, but it was definitely worth it. The doorbell rang downstairs, tempting her to answer it, but she sat down on her bed instead. There was still one more thing to do. Flipping the pages of her worn leather Bible open, she began to read, letting the words sink down into her heart.

"'Do not worry about tomorrow, for tomorrow will worry about itself,'" she read aloud. She smiled. Daddy and God had both known just what she needed. She couldn't have been in better hands.

She shut the Bible and tucked it into her side table drawer, then started downstairs. Before she had even come down the last step, Jade ran up to her and threw her arms around her legs.

"Hi, big girl!" Kiera exclaimed and took the little girl in her arms.

Mom and Brennan were standing behind her, eyes smiling.

"I hash peshent," Jade said, pointing to the small bag Mom was holding. She pulled at her curls and loosened her tiny ponytail beyond recognition.

"She means to say she has a present for you," Mom explained.

"Oh, really?" Kiera turned to Jade. "Should I open

it?"

"Um…yesh," Jade replied characteristically and squirmed out of her arms to go get the present.

Mom gave it to her with an amused smile and watched as the little girl struggled to carry it over to Kiera.

Holding it up proudly, Jade waited for her babysitter to take it. "Now you openen it!"

Kiera sat down on the bottom step. Jade settled in next to her with her chubby legs sticking out straight in front of her. Folding her hands in her lap, she looked up at Kiera with such an expectant, darling face that the older girl couldn't resist planting a kiss on her sunny curls.

Pulling the crumpled tissue paper out of the bag, Kiera saw a small wad of paper tucked in one corner. From two years of babysitting Jade and several of her own nieces and nephews, she knew toddlers well and guessed this must be the "peshent". She smoothed out the paper to find the line drawing they had done together last Saturday.

"Thank you, Jade!" she said, smiling and hugging the little girl.

"We puts it with the peoples?"

Kiera cocked her head.

"With the magnet," Jade added.

"On the refrigerator?"

Jade nodded and the ponytail holder fell out of her hair.

Kiera stooped to pick it up, and Jade took off for the kitchen, picture in hand. Kiera raced after her, and they stood together at the refrigerator. Jade stretched and put it up as high as she could reach, just below the family pictures, then clapped her dimpled hands together, saying, "Ta-da!"

"Ta-da! Where did you learn that, cutie?" Kiera laughed.

"She's been using it all week." Brennan grinned sideways.

Kiera smiled and shook her head. "Every time I see her it seems like she knows half a dozen more words."

Jade held on to Kiera's skirt.

"I'll pick her up after lunch or a little earlier, if I can," Brennan said, ruffling his daughter's mass of curls.

"Don't hurry. This is one of the only days you get to yourself, and you should take it easy," Kiera answered.

Brennan smiled. "I'll try."

When he was gone, she turned to Jade. "Are you ready to play now?"

"Um…yesh." Jade slipped her hand into her babysitter's.

"Don't forget to let me know if you need help with anything," Kiera reminded Mom as they left the room.

Mom smiled. "All right. Have fun, you two!"

CHAPTER FOUR
Wishes

Kiera slowly turned the cake stand as she helped Jade ice the cake with creamy chocolate frosting. It was interesting work directing a two-year-old full of her own ideas and the high possibility of falling off the chair, but it was worth every moment to have the little girl help her. The sweet smell of barbecue smoke wafted through the screen door from the backyard where Dad and Mom were preparing dinner.

She set the bowl of frosting down and put the spreader in the sink. "Ready for sprinkles?"

"Yay! Sprinkles!" Jade clapped her hands together, and Kiera imitated her.

They tossed them onto the frosting like confetti and ate the extras that accidentally hit the counter instead.

"Yummy, yummy, yummy!" Kiera said, popping one into her mouth.

"Nommy, nommy, nommy!" Jade said in a silly,

growly voice and tipped her head back, dropping sprinkles into her mouth. She caught Kiera's eye and they both giggled.

"All right, I think we are all done, so now…" Kiera began. She dusted off Jade's oversized apron and sat her down on the desk chair. "Now we lick the bowl."

Jade clapped again as she handed her the frosting bowl. Putting one short arm all the way around the bowl, she reached deep down into it and gathered up frosting in her fist. Kiera watched in amusement and decided a picture was in order.

Positioning the device where it would catch the borrowed apron with the ties doubled around the toddler's waist, the huge frosting bowl being scraped by chocolatey fingers, and her contented face framed by a wild mass of curls, Kiera snapped the picture just before the doorbell rang.

Jade looked up with big, excited eyes. "Daddy?"

"Maybe, or maybe Destiny. Stay right there for a minute, okay, Jade?" Kiera waited for the sticky nod and took her own apron off.

"Is that the Moores?" Mom called through the open screen door.

"I'm just about to go see," Kiera answered.

She opened the door to birthday wishes and hugs from her best friend, Destiny. Mr. and Mrs. Moore gave her a warm, polite greeting before coming further inside to talk to Dad and Mom.

"Happy birthday, Kiera," Kent said, his dark eyes catching hers.

"Thank you, Kent," she returned with a little smile. "And hello, Aric. If you all want to set that stuff down in the kitchen, that would be great."

Destiny's younger brothers drifted into the kitchen, leaving the two girls in the entryway.

"I am so excited, girly! Now you're old like me, though you're not quite caught up, but eighteen is probably the hugest most ginormous birthday of your life. I have just the thing to help you celebrate." Destiny's words tumbled out. She pulled a stack of sparkly party hats out of her extra large blue purse. "Ta-da!"

"That has to be where Jade learned it!" Kiera exclaimed, snapping her fingers in realization. "But, party hats?"

"You, my dear, are on the threshold between childhood and adulthood. Enjoy yourself one more time before the bills and responsibilities pile up on top of you," Destiny said dramatically, settling her own hat over her poofy black curls. It perfectly complemented her blush-pink blouse and fashionable jeans.

Kiera swallowed at the truth in her best friend's words and decided to enter into the spirit. She took the party hat and put it on at a jaunty angle. "How's that?"

"Properly celebratory," Destiny pronounced, rolling her *r*'s.

"Do you have one for Jade?"

"I have one for everyone. Where is she?"

"In the kitchen, licking out the frosting bowl."

Destiny shrieked over the tiny helper with her chocolate-smeared face and birthday hat. More pictures were necessary, and she and Kiera posed a few times with the chocolate-covered cutie, even convincing the boys to join them. They were just posing for an elaborate and hilarious picture when the doorbell rang. Again.

Kiera moved away for a moment to look out the front blinds. "That would be Brennan," she declared, and the picture party immediately broke up.

Destiny jerked off her undersized hat and reached for Kiera's, but the birthday girl had already hurried off to open the door.

"Hello. Jade's in the kitchen. She's been enjoying licking out the frosting bowl after helping make the cake, but I can get her cleaned up in just a second. But the Moores are here, so if you want to say hey to them real quick…" She trailed off as she led him into the house.

"No problem." He glanced at her hat. "Happy birthday, by the way."

"Thanks."

They paused in the kitchen doorway, and Jade looked up at them with an absolutely melting smile. "Daddy!" She shoved the bowl off her lap and started to get down from the chair.

"Aric, catch her!" Kiera said, rushing forward. "Jade, we gotta get the sticky off you first, okay?"

Jade rubbed at her smudgy cheeks as Kiera picked her up and carried her over to the sink. The others moved out of her way and leaned against the counters, admiring the cake and laughing over the near escape of the toddler.

"Kiera, there's chocolate on her foot too. Want me to wipe it off?" Kent came over to the sink.

"Sure thing. Thanks." She gave him a shy smile before turning back to Jade. "There you go, big girl," she said to the toddler and gave her a light kiss on the forehead.

"All ready to go, Jade?" Brennan appeared next to them and smiled down at his little daughter.

"Yep," Kiera answered for her, looking up at him. "Although if you'd wait a moment, I could grab the book you loaned me. I finished it last night."

"Sure thing." Jade reached for him, and Kiera handed her over.

Hurrying upstairs, she opened her closet door and headed straight for the bookshelf. Brennan's book was on top, and she picked it up, tucking it under her arm.

"Here it is." She reentered the conversation and held the book out.

Brennan took it. "Thanks. What did you think of it?"

"I loved it." An involuntary smile shone on her face as she searched for words. "The allegory was so strong. At first I didn't think I would like it because of how dark it was, but in the end... Thanks for letting me borrow it."

"You're welcome. It's been an important one to me," Brennan said, sliding it into the ever-present diaper bag. "I'll loan you the next one if you like."

"There are more? I'd love that."

"Yes, seven, I think. Well, I'll leave you to your party. Thanks for watching her, Kiera."

"You're welcome! Thanks for the loan of your sunshine. Bye, Jade! See you tomorrow!" She gave a little wave.

"Bye-bye!" Jade gave a little wave and blew a kiss.

They all waved as the Stewarts left, and Destiny blew a kiss herself for good measure.

"How many things have you taught her?" Kiera laughed as she rinsed her hands and dried them on the dish towel.

"Not as many as you have." Destiny pretended to pout. "Lucky girl, getting her twice a week."

"I didn't realize a book club was part of the arrangement," Kent said, coming over to stand next to Kiera. He crossed his arms over his graphic tee.

"Brennan owns different books than I do, and he's very kind to loan them to me," Kiera said, squeezing her thumb. She turned quickly to Destiny. "Ready to make cosmetics?"

"Yep. Boys, this is your warning." Destiny waved the dish towel like a revolutionary flag. "Beet powder and charcoal will be flying. The backyard is your refuge. Basically, run."

The boys edged out of the kitchen with mock-frightened faces.

"Well, that worked," Kiera said, wiping the counter with a wet cloth.

"You can take your birthday hat off now," Destiny said, eyeing it. "Do you realize you were wearing it the whole time Brennan was here?"

"I thought we were being kids and not embarrassed by anything. Besides, it's not like wearing a birthday hat disqualifies you from being a babysitter." Kiera grinned to herself as she helped her friend unpack the ingredients.

"You only care about babysitting, huh?" Destiny gave her a sideways glance.

Kiera snorted and shook her head at her friend. A moment later she shrieked and jumped back from a nearly disastrous spill of the very-staining beet powder. Both girls scrambled to clean it up.

"Wow, your threat was really true," Aric said from the kitchen doorway.

They laughed even harder at his words.

"When you can breathe, Kier, your mom sent me in for cheese for the burgers. Any idea where that would be?" He shoved his hands deep into his pockets, and his dark eyes shone playfully.

Kent and Mrs. Moore came inside with similar questions, and the kitchen was busier than an airport for the next several minutes. Destiny and Kiera finished labeling the tiny cosmetic jars and set them aside before following their families outdoors to the picnic table.

Kiera sat down on a bench, and Destiny and Kent slid in on either side of her. Aric found himself an old lawn chair that kept nearly tipping over through no fault of its own, and the adults pulled up dining chairs brought from the house by the ever-willing boys.

"You sure know how to pick the best meal ever!" Good old Destiny, happily talking with her mouth full.

Kiera nodded toward Mom. "It wasn't my idea. It was hers, and the best idea she's ever had, I think."

"You all are going to kill me with flattery someday," Mom protested. "Try aiming some of that at the grillmasters." She inclined her head toward Dad and Mr. Moore, who both tried to look innocent.

They all shared a laugh that grew even harder as Aric finally succeeded in tipping his chair over. Mom helped him up and commissioned him to give her a hand serving dessert. Kiera turned her head to watch them bring out the cake and felt Kent's eyes on her again. Her only response was to tuck the thought away and gather up enough breath to blow out all the candles.

She needed this wish to come true.

CHAPTER FIVE
In the World

"Did Thorne ever tell you what he was preaching on?" Dad asked, programming the car's destination into the screen at the center of the steering wheel.

"Being 'in the world but not of it'," Kiera replied matter-of-factly from the back seat, but she shifted the folds of her floral skirt nervously.

Dad and Mom exchanged glances.

"He claims it's not purposely; that's just where he is in the text and of course he can't skip it." The car accelerated, and she caught her Bible just before it slid off the seat.

"Our church's hearts grow even harder every week it seems. I'm still wondering when they'll try to vote him out," Dad answered, shaking his head.

"Except that most of the leadership still agree with him. They'll have to pull some strings to get him out anytime soon," Mom said, adjusting her headcovering in the small pocket mirror she always carried.

"Which leaves him in an interesting position. He can say whatever he wants, but that doesn't mean it will have any effect," Kiera sighed, looking out the side window. The traffic had thinned around them, and the car slowed down as they approached the church parking lot.

"Hmmm," Dad said thoughtfully, but he fell silent as he switched the car back to manual and guided it into a vacant parking place.

Kiera pushed these thoughts aside and craned her neck to see if the Moores had arrived yet. The moment the engine powered down, she pulled on her sweater and opened the side door. Following her parents toward the church doors, she noticed Mom still looked a little worried. *Please help it to be all right.*

The greeters at the door gave them a cheerful good morning, and they joined the other worshippers in the crowded lobby. Kiera spied Destiny across the room and smiled immediately.

Weaving her way toward her friend, she said without preamble, "You have something hilarious to tell me, don't you?"

"No, this is just my regular face." Destiny tried to swallow her smile.

They burst into giggles at the same time. Kiera waited for her friend to catch her breath. "Now tell me. What happened?"

Destiny dropped her voice to a whisper. "I spilled beet powder on the carpet this morning. The boys will not let me live it down!"

"Again? Oh, dear. Serves us right for threatening them," Kiera laughed as she entered the sanctuary.

"You're coming to the rally tonight, right?"

"Yep, and I think you all are coming to our house in between so you don't have to drive all the way home to the farm and back again."

"Ooo! Two days in a row. That's Christmas!" Destiny said, making her laugh again.

The girls parted ways with a little wave, and she slid into the pew next to Mom. Thorne took his place at the pulpit to open them in prayer, and she gave him an encouraging smile. Moments later the music began, and she was swept into worship where no worries or fears could touch her. God was bigger than everything. God was here.

Then Thorne began to preach. His voice carried throughout the building all the way to the back where visitors leaned against the wall and tired parishioners refilled their coffee cups. He flowed from thought to thought effortlessly, keeping her attention so well she hardly noticed the dissenting looks scattered across the crowd.

He began with showing how Christ was separate from the world but a minister to it, then moved into practical applications for everyone. Her pen flew across her notebook page. Here was something that applied to her as a daughter, a sister, a friend, and even a babysitter.

The thought of babysitting jerked her attention toward the Stewarts' pew, and she realized Brennan was signaling her. He pointed to a squirming Jade and out the back doors to the lobby. She nodded and slipped across the aisle to lead the little girl out of the sanctuary. They reached the ladies' room in record time, but Jade characteristically stalled as soon as the potty seat was in place.

The women of the church had put together a rotation of people to babysit Jade while her dad was at work, but the extras like Bible study night, errand day, and times like this always seemed to fall to Kiera. Not that she minded.

Kiera leaned against the stall door and crossed her arms to wait. Jade looked up at her, and she made sure to offer a patient smile. They were still waiting when a few ladies entered the room and broke the silence.

"...but that's just too radical. How will we be able to reach out to others if we look like we're from a whole other country or time period?"

"He has a too judgmental view of things, and my husband, for one, isn't going to stand for it any longer. Everyone should only use nice, kind words all the time? I don't think that's even possible."

Kiera's cheeks burned as she recognized the voices of two deacons' wives. She wished Jade would hurry so she wouldn't have to hear any more critical, skewed words. That was not what Thorne had said. He was only speaking out against the use of foul language as the people of God. She prayed they would stop talking soon.

"Apparently, in their last meeting, Thorne got on his high horse. Deacon White and Deacon Tiegler sided with him."

The other woman spoke. "I don't see how we'll ever be able to vote him out, but I'm not sure I can take this negativity any longer."

"Don't worry, dear. God is already providing a way."

The voices continued and, as a last resort, Kiera put her earbuds in, leaving the end of the cord in her purse. Jade finished up soon enough, and the two astonished women paused in their conversation as Kiera Clark emerged from the stall and wordlessly helped her little charge wash her hands.

Kiera's stomach churned as she marched into the lobby. She stuffed the earbuds back into her purse and entered the sanctuary. Thorne was just closing the service in prayer, so she sat down in Brennan's row with Jade on her lap. The less noise she made during the prayer the better. She only hoped the thumping of her anxious heart wasn't loud enough for anyone to hear.

"Aric, get us that one Kiera's crazy about, whatever it's called. Please?" Destiny said over the sound of the blender. She measured popcorn kernels into a pan.

"Kier, what's it called?" Aric asked from the desk. He had cleared a spot to sit on and absentmindedly kicked the desk chair with his foot to make it spin.

There was a pause in the blending. "'Sparrows'. The original version by Jason Gray."

Aric scratched his ear and searched through the music library.

Kiera tasted the smoothie she and Kent were making together. "I think it needs a little more ice and then it'll be just perfect," she told him.

Kent opened the freezer. "Ice coming right up."

"Thank you, kind sir." She dumped in a few cubes and gave the blender another whirl.

She was just pouring the chocolate smoothie into canning jars he retrieved for her when Aric finally found her song. From the very first notes, happiness surged up inside of her, making the white kitchen cabinets and the smiles of her friends seem even brighter. Kent grabbed her hands and spun her around in a circle.

They slammed into the island, and the laughter stayed on her cheeks as she turned back to the smoothies. The words of the song seeped into her as she set the smoothies on a tray and carried them into the living room.

She passed the tray around, and they each took one, exclaiming over how good they looked.

"Kent helped me," she explained.

"Oh, did he?" Mrs. Moore said with an open-mouthed smile and took a sip. Her black curls were tied up with an exotic orange headband.

"Aric behaving himself?" Mr. Moore asked. He seemed on edge.

Kiera caught Mom's encouraging look as she spoke. "He's completely in charge of music and doing a great job. We won't let him do anything else."

"Katie, that reminds me." Mrs. Moore laid a hand on Mom's arm. "Kent and Destiny want Kiera to ride with us, but we don't have enough seats. Could you take Aric in your vehicle?"

After a quick exchange with Dad, she answered, "Yes, that would be all right."

"It's about time to start out anyway," Dad said, rising and grinning toward the kitchen. "Looks like we'll have to interrupt a popcorn war, though."

All the cooks were delighted to ride together, but Kiera noticed Aric's disappointment as he got in the car with her parents. "Poor guy. I know what it's like to be the youngest," she remarked when the car had started.

"We'll make sure to stand with him at the rally," Destiny assured her.

They jostled each other around, fitting themselves, coats, and a random purse or two into the narrow back seat. Kiera leaned against Destiny to let Kent strap himself in and caught a glimpse of Mr. Moore in the reflection of the car screen. His eyebrows were pulled together in a frown, and he mumbled something darkly under his breath to his wife. Kiera didn't like what she saw, but she knew it wasn't any of her concern.

"You all comfortable back there?" Mrs. Moore asked brightly.

"Sardine-ish, but good," Destiny called back.

They spent the rest of the drive discussing how "sardines" sounded like they were a band and what type of music they would play.

"We might make it big, but what if people think our idea is fishy?" Destiny said.

Kent burst out in a chuckle and reached behind Kiera to pull one of Destiny's curls. Destiny gasped in mock frustration and punched him on the shoulder. Kiera leaned forward, unable to hold in her laughter.

"Would you three be quiet back there?" Mr. Moore slapped the steering wheel and his hand formed into a fist. "We're trying to talk."

Kiera shrank back.

"Dad, we were only ignoring your argument like you tell us to so often," Kent said levelly.

"It's not an argument, okay?" Mr. Moore burst out again. He muttered an expletive.

Destiny was silent, staring into nothing.

"Louis, not now. We have a guest," Mrs. Moore said gently, though her eyes were fire.

The engine slowed to a stop, and the doors clicked unlocked. "We're here," Mr. Moore said. "Get out.

We'll join you later."

Destiny opened the door so quickly she almost fell out, and Kiera and Kent hurried after her.

Industrial buildings rose up around a parking lot that was full to the brim with self-driving cars. Here and there an old manual with peeling paint stood out. Music came from loudspeakers at the far end of the parking lot, and a large crowd swelled and stirred around it.

Destiny walked ahead, and Kiera hurried to catch up with her.

"I'm sorry," Destiny mumbled, shifting her bracelets up and down her arm.

"It's okay. People have bad days sometimes," Kiera said, giving her a side hug. She felt her friend relax.

Behind them, Kent kicked a biodegradable bottle aside. "You didn't see anything. You should see it when they really fight."

"Kent, please don't," Destiny said, closing her eyes as if she had a headache.

"They didn't want you to see, you being the pastor's sister and all, the hypocrites," Kent went on. He laughed, but his hands were clenched. "We should keep you around more often."

They fell silent as they neared the crowd and joined the edge of it. A breeze blew across the parking lot, helping Kiera calm herself. She sent up a short prayer for the Moores and gave Destiny another hug.

Kent stood close to her, his shoulder almost touching hers.

"Thank you all for joining us today to celebrate the gift of life and defend those who are unable to speak for themselves." Thorne's voice came through the loudspeakers, powerful yet gentle. "I'll open us in a word of prayer, and then I'll turn it over to Jessica. She'll be laying out the goals and rules for this event."

Kiera gave Destiny a conspiratorial glance and was glad to see her friend returned it.

"Our Father in Heaven, hallowed be Thy Name…"

It was the only prayer they were allowed to say in public. Someone had managed to get it approved as an ancient literary "poem".

"Amen. All right, Jessica, would you fill us in on the instructions?" Thorne handed her the microphone.

Jessica stepped up to the edge of the stage and hand-combed her long bangs out of her eyes. Her smile shone more than the fashionable boots she wore. "Thank you, Pastor Thorne. And thank you all for coming out today. Our goal for this event is to remind people every life is precious and to pray for them while we do it."

Jessica switched the microphone to her other hand. "Instruction number one is don't engage with passersby with hand signals, gestures, or words. Keep it to smiles, please. Secondly, please only use one of the approved signs. We've been working with the local government for weeks to have these signs approved, and any others could have us removed from the premises. And last, I'd like to introduce Officers Dean, Koontz, and Lund."

Three officers filed onto the stage, looking as if they wondered what they were doing there. Kiera wondered herself. The last rally hadn't been this closely monitored.

"They have been assigned to escort us and see that no harm comes to any person or the premises. Please treat them with respect and follow their instructions. That's all I have to say, so I'm trading off to Pastor Thorne again."

"Thank you, Jessica," Thorne said. "All right, everyone line up and walk this way. You can pick up your signs on the way to the streetside."

Mom, Dad, and Aric pushed their way through the crowd and joined them in line. They shifted forward slowly but soon reached the table where the signs were set out. Officer Lund stood casually near the table, staring over the heads of the people and listening to his radio.

Kiera looked at the signs. One said "God loves you" and the other said "All life is precious". They seemed trivial in light of the heartrending issue at hand, but this rally was only meant to be a conversation starter. In a fast-changing world, she was suddenly grateful they were able to say anything at all.

CHAPTER SIX
Anchor

Kiera opened the sliding glass door and slipped out into the yard. The raw afternoon sunlight met her full in the face, and she pushed it aside with a shading hand. She wandered over to her raised garden beds. Her fingertips brushed the cool soil as she spoke aloud.

"There's nothing wrong with me, I know it. The doctors didn't say anything when they examined me, but I could tell." She gripped the wooden side of the box. Splinters grated at her palms. "Mom could too."

Kiera looked toward the dusty glass door. She could just see the outlines of Dad and Mom in the dining room. Their arms were around each other, and she knew they were praying.

"I know…" She stopped with a voice full of tears and looked up at the sky. "I know You are good. I know that if You don't want me to be drafted, You'll send us a way. I was sure You'd use the physical examination as a way out. But now, I don't know what You're doing."

She opened her mouth to speak but realized there was nothing more to say. Thoughts and emotions seemed far away and only actions remained. Kiera brushed the dirt from her fingers and drifted into the house. Mom and Dad were still praying together, and she gave them a grateful look as she walked by into the kitchen.

The heartbeat rhythm of the manual clock greeted her as she turned on the faucet to rinse lettuce. She patted the leaves dry with a kitchen towel. Chopped them into the glass salad bowl. Prepared every topping she could find until the salad was as full as a thick sandwich. Throwing the scraps into a compost bin under the sink, she sat down at the device to take a break.

She stared at the screen, idly sliding her finger in circles to make the apps dance. Her public journaling app hadn't been updated since her birthday the weekend before, but she didn't feel like telling her readers the latest news.

She had no health problems. Her last chance for exemption was gone. In that second her fingers froze on the keyboard and reality hit her again. All of the tears she had cried returned, and she covered her face with both hands in an effort to keep them back. A little sob escaped from her throat, and Mom rushed into the kitchen to pull her into a hug. "Oh, Kiera, honey. It's going to be all right."

She could barely speak through her tears, but she tried to apologize for the outburst. Dad came over to join them and began to hum as he stroked her hair.

"Sparrow, don't apologize. You're exhausted. You should go upstairs and rest for a while," he said gently.

"I'll finish dinner, dear. And you can come down to eat it whenever you want," Mom added.

"Thank you," Kiera said, smiling at them. "I'll try."

"Our God is able."

These words fixed themselves in her mind and repeated over and over like a lullaby until she fell into a deep sleep.

Kiera jerked awake and sat up. Why was she sleeping on top of her blankets in the middle of the day? Was that the front door she had heard? She stretched, staring blankly down at the wrinkles ironed into her dress. The front door shut, and she panicked. Bible study night. Jade was coming.

Pausing to smooth down her staticky hair and shake some of the wrinkles out of her clothes, she hurried downstairs to find Mom washing the dinner dishes.

"Did Brennan come?" she asked, frantically looking around the quiet house for signs of visitors.

"Yes, he brought Jade by. She's in the backyard playing dolls with your father." A smile slipped onto

Mom's face. "She's named him Clock, since apparently Mr. Clark is too hard to say."

"That's so cute," Kiera answered, taking out a pan to reheat dinner leftovers. With Jade temporarily busy, she had a little time to eat something. "You didn't tell Brennan I had a meltdown, right?"

"Of course not," Mom said, a laugh shining in her eyes.

"Good," Kiera replied with her mouth half-full as she spun in the desk chair and ate her dinner. The cheese on her lasagna was crunchy from reheating. Just how she liked it.

"I told him what happened today, though, and he promised to pray for a solution." Mom watched her carefully as she said these words.

Kiera nodded solemnly and spun around in her chair again. She soon finished her lasagna and was just scraping the last bite from her plate when Jade appeared.

"Hi! I hash dollies like last night." Jade came up to her.

"Hi, big girl! Nice dollies," she said, pausing to admire the three dolls Jade held out to her. She looked up at Dad and gave him a grateful grin.

"This is Mary and this is Jobie—no, this one is Jobie and dat one is Mary." Jade juggled the dolls in her arms and tried to introduce them by their new names.

"Oh, and what's the name of that one?" she asked,

pointing to the third doll, formerly named Boo.

"Um, she doesn't hash one." Jade shrugged.

Kiera laughed and led the tiny girl to the living room. They spread out an old floral sheet and set out the play tea set Kiera had used as a little girl. The wooden plates and cups, teapot and sugar bowl, all painted in bright yellow and pink, brought back sweet memories.

"We all needs cups, even the dollies," Jade decided, scooting the sugar bowl up to Jobie. The doll flopped forward against it, her black hair a tangle of frizz.

Kiera propped a doll up against her knees. As she watched Jade pass out imaginary tea sandwiches, the tears filled her eyes again. In another fifteen years, would this precious little girl be facing the same fears and worries?

"Eat!" Jade said, pointing to the tiny plate in front of her babysitter.

"Oh, what food do I have?" Kiera managed a smile for her little friend.

"Mac an' cheese, ice cream, cookies…" Jade shrugged again and her eyebrows danced up and down.

"And pickles?"

"Ummmm…sure." She grabbed an imaginary pickle off the serving plate and put it on Kiera's.

Kiera pretended to groan from how full she was going to be. They ate together, taught the dollies a new song, and ate some more. Jade grew sleepy and stretched out on the "picnic blanket" with a yawn.

"Are you sleepy, Jade?" Kiera asked, leaning down and looking at her.

Jade shook her head but didn't sit up. Kiera lifted her onto the couch, tucking the dollies in around her.

"I hash blanket?" Jade mumbled around her thumb.

Kiera spread the soft pink blanket over her and leaned down to give her a hug. "Thanks for playing with me."

Jade didn't answer. She was already asleep.

Kiera scooped the tea set back into its box and set it aside. Stopping off in the kitchen to grab a drink of water, she took the device with her, deciding to attempt updating the journal again. She sat down with her back against the couch and put her earbuds in. She titled the journal entry "Our God Is Able", then replaced His name with a "code word".

Posts containing the usual names of God on a public journal were either blocked or deleted, so she had to find ways to get past this. What would she use this time? She glanced at the peacefully sleeping Jade and decided on the word *anchor*.

She had let her fears overwhelm her earlier, but God wouldn't let her forget He was still working. There hadn't been a large miracle or a direct answer to her prayers. Instead, His peace had come to her through the help of her parents and the joys of Jade.

Kiera was so busy pouring her thoughts onto the page, skimming the lotion recipe Mom had bookmarked for her, and reading another crazy reply from Destiny that she didn't notice Brennan's arrival until he was standing directly in front of her. She jumped visibly and took out her earbuds.

"Hello! Sorry. I didn't hear you knock," she said, moving the device off her lap and standing up quickly. How long had he been standing there?

"Oh, that's fine. Don't worry about it." He glanced at her, then looked away. "Your parents let me in, obviously." He tried to sound casual, but she could tell something was on his mind.

"Okay, yeah." She smiled and nodded, then moved to pack the diaper bag.

Brennan stooped down to pick up Jade, and she melted against him, thumb falling out of her mouth. Her eyes began to flicker open, but he shifted her to a comfortable position and she drifted back to sleep.

Brennan looked at Kiera, and she realized she'd been watching them. Something in the back of her mind wanted to know what he was thinking, but she didn't ask. She picked up the heavy diaper bag and handed it to him.

"Thanks," he said, barely looking at her.

"You're welcome."

Kiera opened the door for him, and he stepped outside but turned around on the porch. "Hey, I just wanted to say that I know what you're going through."

He stopped, looking almost startled with himself for choosing to speak.

Kiera waited. His eyes looked tired, and he used a tone she had never heard from him before.

"When I first knew Jade would be mine, I felt alone and afraid. There was uncertainty and some hard decisions. God's done a lot in my life through it though, and He's shown Himself to me through people." He shifted Jade on his shoulder. "No matter what happens, I want you to know there are people who care about you and are praying for a solution."

Kiera let her eyes drop and squeezed her thumb tightly. Her words were so quiet she wasn't sure he could hear them. "Thank you."

She shut the front door and turned to see Dad and Mom sitting on the couches in the living room. Mom patted the couch next to her and said calmly, "Kiera, honey, we have something we need to share with you."

CHAPTER SEVEN
Decisions

Kiera settled herself down on the couch next to Mom.

"When I was a kid, turning eighteen meant a lot of good things. Adulthood was exciting. New opportunities, privileges, the option to vote." Dad folded his fingers together and studied the carpet in front of him. He looked up at Kiera. "I realize for you adulthood means many other things, some not as good. Some hard decisions."

His words were so close to what Brennan had said. But what decision did she have? There was no way out of the draft. The government was deciding for her. Mom's arm curled around her, and she snuggled in, waiting for Dad's next words.

"Brennan heard the news just like everyone else did, and he asked Thorne what we were going to do. Today, when he dropped Jade off, he asked us what the results of your examination were."

Kiera's stomach pitched at the thought. Had it

only been this morning when she'd been scrutinized by doctors?

Dad's voice faltered, and Mom picked up the story. "When he came by this evening to get Jade, he seemed very anxious. He told us that, while he was praying, God had opened his heart to a solution."

Kiera sat up straighter and stared at Mom. She turned her eyes on Dad, squeezing both thumbs in anticipation. The silence hung heavy. "Well, what was his idea?"

"Kiera." Dad leaned forward and answered her question with another. "What do you think of Brennan?"

She shrugged. "Um, he's a great guy. Thorne respects him, which is saying a lot. He's good with Jade and brave to adopt her. I don't know." She released her thumbs. The conversation seemed to be taking another turn. "Why do you ask?"

"Brennan Stewart has offered to marry you."

Kiera's mouth dropped open. "Wait, why? How does that help anything? Why him? If anyone was interested in me, I thought it would be Kent."

"Brennan's last name alone isn't enough to protect you from the draft, but marrying him would make you Jade's mother, and mothers are exempt. That's why Niyanna doesn't have to go. You would have to move in with them to prove your change of status on paper."

Jade's mother. Jade's *mother*. The words skated around in her brain.

"He doesn't expect a yes, and he would be all right with a no. Kiera, Brennan is offering this only to help you. It would be a paper marriage and nothing more. He wants you to know he doesn't expect anything of you."

Dad and Mom were on either side of her now. Arms wrapped around her. This would solve everything. Wouldn't it?

"You don't need to give your answer right away, of course. It's a hard decision, and it's all yours to make," Mom said, a weak smile playing on her lips.

"But we're here for you, and we'll be praying."

Brennan had said there were people praying for her. Was he one of them?

Kiera grimaced at herself in the bathroom mirror to see if her teeth were clean enough yet. They looked pretty good. She stretched her lip away from her teeth and checked the base of her gums just to be sure. Satisfied, she rinsed her toothbrush and put it away in the medicine cabinet.

As she turned away, she noticed acne forming along the edge of her hairline and decided to treat it before it flared up even more. The thought struck her again. Brennan Stewart had offered to marry her—a girl just barely out of high school who still had meltdowns, breakouts, and occasionally even nightmares.

After a whole night and a day of thinking about it, she still couldn't believe this was actually real. Even worse, she still couldn't decide what she thought of it. A paperwork wedding. No butterflies. No romance. Forever. He only wanted to protect her from the draft.

She sighed and entered her bedroom, folding her comforter back and sitting down cross-legged, unwilling to settle down to the long night just yet. Her lamp glowed next to her, warm light filtering through the linen shade. She cradled her chin in her hands and thought back on the day.

Ever since the night before, she and her parents had talked and prayed, prayed and talked, and prayed some more. Dad had even stayed home from work to stay in the discussion. Thorne shared his opinion of Brennan as his closest friend.

God had given all three of them a peace that this was within His will. The nervous ache in her stomach was gone, and she found herself hungry for the dinner she had skipped. But one question remained in her mind. Was she willing to take the name of a man who would likely never love her?

Kiera smiled wryly. It sounded a bit like an odd soap opera or the beginning of one of the romance novels Destiny had loaned her. It was a hard decision only because she was the one making it.

"Talk about opportunity cost," she sighed and slid under her blankets.

She had always known what her wedding would

look like. Not in colors or dresses or diamonds or flowers, but in her heart. Love and excitement. She felt none of that at the moment, just confusion.

Rolling over, her thoughts took a new turn. This was her only way out. Her only chance at safety and survival. And Brennan really was a good guy. Better than most. He was easy to talk to and a small corner of her heart *was* warm toward him.

Kiera sat up and threw her blankets to the floor. This was getting her nowhere. Slipping on her shoes, she stepped into the closet and yanked her coat off its hanger. Buttoning it on over her nightgown, she went downstairs.

Mom and Dad looked up from the kitchen table, surprise showing plainly on their faces.

"Would it be all right if I went outside for a moment? I can't sleep at all."

Dad nodded and she made a beeline for the back door without another word.

The night air was cold. A few brave stars shone through the pollution, and the crisp breeze lifted Kiera's light-brown hair and shivered down her neck. Walking over to the toolshed, she slipped off her shoes. She lifted one foot to the windowsill, then the other, and pulled herself up onto the roof. The fiberglass shingles felt rough against her legs, but she leaned back and stretched her arms above her head.

"Lord, I don't know what to do, I—" Not good. She was sliding. Kiera grabbed the rain gutter and pushed herself back up the slope of the roof. Her fingers brushed something sharp and tangled. Jerking back, she kicked herself for not bringing a flashlight.

"It better not be something spidery." She leaned forward to look, her tangled hair falling over her shoulders. The outline of the something was barely clear, but she drew it out of the rain gutter, shook it over the grass for spiders, and then examined it more closely.

A bird's nest. Perfectly round. Perfectly prickly. "Did we have birds here? I never saw them, but I like to imagine they were sparrows."

A little smile quirked the corner of her mouth. "I'm Your sparrow, aren't I? You're good, whatever happens, I know that. I've seen it." Kiera fixed her eyes on one bright star as if looking at it would help her see beyond to heaven. "It's just that right now, You've given me a choice, and I don't know what to do with it. I'm lonely just thinking about spending the rest of my life like that."

Her face grew wistful as she ran her fingers along the edge of the nest. The wind picked up and she shivered, hunching herself into her coat and plunging her free hand into her pocket. A curl of paper met her fingers, and she crunched it, relishing the feel of the corners against her palm.

"I better go in, shouldn't I?" Kiera tucked the nest under her arm and made her way down from the shed roof.

Shoes back on her feet. Padding across the grass. A little more peace in her heart, but not enough.

The porch light glowed yellow on the garden boxes, and she paused to look through the glass door at her parents sitting in the living room.

"What do I do?" she whispered, sliding her hand into her pocket again. A sharp corner of paper jabbed her finger, and she drew it out.

Setting the nest down, she smoothed out the paper and held it up to the light. It was written in Thorne's loopy, hurried handwriting. "'Love is not [merely] affectionate feeling but a steady wish for the loved person's ultimate good as far as it can be obtained,'" Kiera read aloud.

Thorne's Valentine's Day sermon. He had given her the quote afterward. She read it again.

"You wanted me to remember this now, didn't You, Lord?" A tear slid down her cheek and fell into her coat collar.

She had forgotten about it entirely all spring, but now when she needed it He was using a quote by C. S. Lewis to speak to her again.

Kiera tucked the piece of paper into the nest and stared down at it. Brennan did love her. Not in a hearts and roses way, but deeper and Christ-like, which in the end mattered more. If this was love, then she was willing to give it to Brennan and his daughter.

Moments later, she was standing in the living room, both hands wrapped around the nest. Dad and

Mom looked up at her expectantly.

"I have my answer for Brennan." There was no hesitation in her voice.

Her parents scooted apart and motioned for her to sit down with them.

"I was sure about everything except how lonely it would be that he doesn't love me. God showed me differently." Kiera handed them the slip of paper. "I am willing to marry him."

Mom nodded and Dad smiled at her. "Let's pray together," he said.

After more prayer and a short voice call with Thorne, it was time.

"Should I call him or send a message?" Kiera felt nervousness crowding in again.

"See if he's available for a call," Dad encouraged.

Her first message was clumsy. She erased it and tried again, unsure if the second try was better or worse.

Brennan, do you have time for a voice call?

She wasn't sure how to sign off, so she skipped it completely and stared at the wall in front of her while she waited for his reply. Mom slipped her arm around Kiera's shoulders to give her an encouraging squeeze while Dad waited nearby. She refreshed the app, but no reply appeared. The clock showed the time accusingly. It was probably too late to expect an answer.

A reply popped up, and she read it aloud. "Yes. I'll call you."

Moments later, she answered his call and was half relieved to hear the nervousness in his voice. "Hi, Kiera. How are you?"

"I'm doing all right. I, um, wanted to talk about your offer." She looked at Dad, and he gave her a wink.

"Okay. You all talked about it?"

"All last night and today when we weren't busy praying. Oh, and we ate some too." She laughed, trying to sound at ease. "Thank you very much for thinking of it. If you are still sure, I am willing to do this."

"Kiera, I'm sure." His voice softened a little as he added, "The last thing we need is for you to get drafted."

Kiera looked down at the ground. There was the love.

"What time works best for you?"

"We were thinking tomorrow after dinner might be best. That would give me a few hours to pack, and Thorne said he'd be willing to do the honors. If that's good with you."

"That'll work. I'll be over around five with the truck, so we can move all your stuff in one load."

"Okay." She yawned and leaned against Mom. "Jade's coming too?"

"Yes. See you tomorrow, Kiera."

"Bye." The voice call ended, and she shut the device for the night. Tomorrow was a full day. Going to sleep sounded like a great idea right then, but she still had a few things to tell God before her eyes wouldn't stay open.

Kiera scrawled a label on the side of her cardboard box and pushed it out into the loft. She wondered what Destiny would say if she knew what was going on. There hadn't been any time to warn her since the day had been as full as the stack of boxes she had worked through. She grinned to herself and shook her head. Dear flat-footed Destiny would never have to worry about the draft, but she'd be quick to forgive when Kiera showed her the crumpled quote she kept in her hip pocket.

She stood up and shoved the marker into her other pocket, then surveyed the room around her. It was lonely now. Stripped of everything that made it hers. Her desk and dresser, mirror and bookshelf all painted to match were waiting patiently downstairs to take their place in the Stewarts' guest bedroom. Only a white-sheeted bed and side table stood in the middle of the room, looking like a scene from a hospital ward.

Kiera told herself Mom would redecorate it soon enough and her nieces and nephews would add a spark of life to it whenever they visited. Crossing the room, she stood at the window and pulled back the gauzy curtain. The yard looked small from this high, and she could see the thick branches of the big trees in the neighbor's yard. She had already taken her seashells and the bird's nest out of her windowsill, leaving only dust and a forgotten bobby pin as she shut the door behind her on so many memories.

Dad was waiting in the loft when she appeared, stray tears on her cheeks. She gestured toward her bedroom. "It's silly, but I was just...saying goodbye. I think I've had that room forever."

He smiled and nodded gently. "I checked the forecast. No rain to spoil your boxes in the back of the truck." He gestured toward the last box. "Brennan and I are just about ready to take the furniture over, but I can squeeze that box in if you like."

Kiera nodded and let him leave without another word. She stayed in the loft until she heard the front door shut. She wasn't ready to face Brennan yet.

Thorne was in the kitchen, tying on a barbecue apron, and she gave him a welcoming hug.

"Heya, Kiera! How's your heart?" he asked.

"I'm doing okay; I'm just not sure what I'm going to do when he gets here. This is something I've never really had to think about before." She grinned for his benefit to assure him she would be okay.

"I'm praying for you." He winked and stepped outside to babysit the burgers, leaving Mom and Kiera to assemble an apple crisp.

"Now, is there anything I can lick?" Kiera asked,

looking mischievously at the various sugary measuring cups they had used.

Mom spanked her playfully with the oven mitt.

"Thanks for being my mom," she said quietly, giving her an impulsive hug.

Mom held her tight for a moment. "Anytime. You'll always be my baby girl."

The doorbell broke in, and her stomach jumped. They were back.

"I'll get it," Mom offered, and Kiera gladly took a moment to pray.

All nervousness vanished away into thin air when Jade appeared in the kitchen and ran straight up to her with a huge smile.

"Hi, big girl!" Kiera exclaimed, scooping her up into a hug.

"I eat?" Jade asked, pointing to the apple crisp in the top oven.

"No," she laughed. "Not yet. You'll have to wait a little longer."

"I eat?" Thorne's voice mimicked behind her.

Her voice held a laugh. "No, but if you two hungry toddlers are willing, you can set the table. Picnic supplies are in the top right cabinet."

"C'mon, Jade, we've been banished," he said, taking the little girl's hand.

Kiera straightened from putting vegetable scraps in the compost can to see Brennan standing in the kitchen doorway.

"Hello," she said before running out of words. She squeezed her thumb and let herself look him full in the face for a moment. Nothing about him had changed. His friendly smile filled her with relief.

"Hello," he replied, running his fingers through his dark brown hair. "Anything I can do to help with dinner?"

CHAPTER EIGHT
Gold

The truck stopped suddenly to avoid an oncoming vehicle, and the lamp between Kiera's feet toppled over. She leaned over the open box on her lap to secure it, then straightened to check on Jade in the back seat. The little girl had fallen asleep with one cheek squished against her car seat and didn't even stir when the truck lurched forward again.

Kiera settled back, brushing her hair out of her face. Her ring sparkled in the light of the solar streetlights, and she twisted the delicate band on her finger. The fine lines engraved into it looked like golden wheat, but the only picture that came to her mind was when Brennan had slipped it onto her finger only hours ago.

Thorne had prayed for them both, and then they had exchanged vows. Solemn promises before God. Brennan holding the tips of her fingers. Like a dancing partner. Nothing more.

She had entirely forgotten there would need to be rings until he took the slender gold band out of his pocket. A flush burned in her cheeks. She didn't have one to give him. Before she could apologize, he had removed the old family ring from his right hand and switched it to his left.

She cleared her throat and clamped her feet around the lamp as the truck turned another corner. "So what does your routine usually look like on Sunday morning?"

Brennan seemed glad the silence was broken. "Oh, there isn't much of one. We usually get up around eight and eat whatever we can find; I leave Jade in her highchair while I get ready. We tend to scramble into the car around ten."

Kiera nodded. She could fit into that. "And," she hesitated, "what do you do after church?" She half-dreaded another time when she would have to drum up a conversation topic.

"Jade takes a nap." He paused to concentrate on the road in front of him for a moment. He grinned and added, "She definitely needs it by then. I'm no Sabbatarian, but I like to rest some myself since Saturday is usually a busy day. I often catch up on Bible reading, read something else, or watch a movie. What about you?" He turned to look at her.

"About the same, though sometimes Destiny has buried me in messages and I take the chance to catch up." She gave a little laugh at the thought and looked out the side window at the neighborhood they were passing by.

"You two are pretty much best friends, aren't you?"

Kiera nodded, turning back to him. "You have one?"

Brennan shrugged. His eyes seemed to dim in the half light. "Not really. School and work have kept me too busy for that, so Thorne and the guys from Bible study are the closest I've had." He ran his fingers through his hair again.

They lapsed into silence, and she twisted her ring on her finger again. It had been more important than she had thought for her to babysit Jade so he could attend Bible study. With his family far away, that group was all he had.

"We're in my neighborhood now." He broke into her thoughts, and she sat up, jostling the lamp again.

The roads were ruler straight with houses evenly spaced along either side of them and a streetlight to illuminate each yard. The only variations between each manufactured model were the cars parked outside of them. Just like her neighborhood.

The truck slowed and turned into the driveway of one house, powering down a few feet from the garage door. The doors unlocked with a click, and the headlights shut off. Kiera unbuckled her seat belt distractedly as she admired the front door. It had been painted a gorgeously original chocolate brown.

She took in every detail as she stood on the driveway and waited for Brennan to get Jade out of her carseat. The night wind whipped through her hair, and she glanced up to see two bright stars shining like the porch lights farther down the street. Hugging the box to herself for warmth, she followed Brennan up to the porch.

"The code is Jade's birth year, or I can get you a key if you prefer," he remarked, unlocking the door and throwing it open.

"I can remember the code," Kiera assured him, stepping into the house.

It was much smaller than her own home, but the tasteful decorating made it feel cozy, not crowded. The kitchen was set apart from the living room by a half wall, and the dining room was beyond it near the back door. She looked to her right and inwardly admired the setup of the light-brown couches, side tables, and a bookshelf that made the living room.

Slipping her shoes off and setting her box on a bench in the entryway, she started forward hesitantly to run her fingers along the spines of the books and straighten a blanket thrown over the arm of one couch. She looked up to see Brennan watching her and gave him a nervous smile.

He inclined his head toward the little girl in his arms. "If you wanted to put Jade to bed, you could explore the house while I start unloading."

Kiera reached out to take the little girl, grateful for

the diversion. "Sounds good," she said quietly, avoiding eye contact. She picked up her small box in the other arm and started upstairs, deciding this was where all the bedrooms would be in such a small house.

The first door was ajar. She pushed it open to find a room that looked right out of a magazine. Definitely not the nursery since there wasn't a crib. Her gaze fell on a pair of construction boots overturned just inside the door. Brennan's room. She turned to the other doors across the loft.

Moments later, she entered her own room, barely furnished and empty of all personality. Just like her room at home now. She set her box on the edge of the bed before turning away to explore the next room over. Jade's. Pink and white and fit for a princess. She sat down in the middle of the floor, letting Jade slump in her lap as she pulled open each dresser drawer, searching for the little girl's pajamas.

When Kiera had her all cozied up in a fluffy sleeper, she hugged her tight and carried her over to the crib. One of them. She looked around the room again and pinched herself. The room had been set up for twins. The only difference between the two cribs was several of Jade's dolls piled high in a corner. The other was empty, the polka-dotted sheet smooth.

She shoved the questions out of her mind and laid Jade down in her crib, smoothing a soft blanket over her. Laying a kiss on the sunny curls, she lingered a moment to watch her sleep peacefully before shutting the door on her daughter's room.

Kiera tiptoed into her own room and over to the window. Soft moonlight and artificial street light filtered in. She pulled the box toward her and took out her seashells. One by one she gently placed them in the windowsill. The bird's nest joined them. She nodded in satisfaction. There was one more thing to do.

Removing the vintage clock from the box, she hugged it to herself as she walked past a growing stack of boxes to the kitchen. A few dishes sat in the stainless steel sink, but the counters were empty for her to choose any spot to place the clock. She set it down and stood back to admire it, running her hands along the smooth edge of the countertop.

The rhythmic ticking filled the entire room like a heartbeat for her own kitchen. A tear slipped down her cheek.

CHAPTER NINE
Settling In

Kiera slipped out the open front door and met Brennan on the porch. Taking a box from him, she carried it to the stack, then stepped outside again. The chill of the night wind tore at her, and she rubbed her upper arms.

"I packed my coat like a dummy," she explained to Brennan.

"I have one in the front closet you can borrow," he offered as he set down a stack of boxes.

It was several sizes too large and smelled dusty, but she was grateful for its warmth as they unloaded the last of the boxes.

"That's everything," Brennan announced, leaning against the island counter.

Kiera looked around the kitchen at the glass-fronted cabinets filled with dishes, the light shades over the window, and the double oven shining at her. She twisted her ring, half-hidden by the long coat sleeve.

"Kiera." Brennan's tone brought her attention to him. "Nothing needs to change between us."

She smiled weakly and nodded. "I know." But it already had.

Kiera stretched to reach under her desk and plug in her lamp. Backing out from under it, she nearly collided with Brennan carrying her mirror. She moved aside, only to bump into one of the boxes that had stolen all the floor space.

"Do you want me to hang this up?" Brennan asked.

Kiera brushed her hair and a few dust bunnies out of her eyes. "Yes. Thank you."

He laid the mirror face down on her bed and set to work putting adhesive strips on the back. She squeezed past him, being careful not to bang her hip into the corner of the desk, and dragged a box marked "Accessories" into the closet. Shoes filled the bottom shelf of her bookshelf, folded sweaters and her winter coat followed, and a few miscellaneous scarves and belts joined them. She broke down each box and propped them against the wall outside her bedroom door.

Brennan had disappeared, but soon returned with a measuring tape to hang the mirror with contractor precision. Kiera carried three boxes of books into the closet and tried to arrange them in a tentative order on her shelves. She was too tired right now to worry if they were alphabetically arranged or even right side up. For all she knew it could already be Sunday morning.

"How's this?" Brennan's voice came through the half-open closet door.

She pushed it open and came over to stand next to him, carefully avoiding looking at them in the mirror together. "I think it's good. Thank you."

"You're welcome. Do you need help with anything else?"

She looked around at the room full of boxes still to be unpacked, the window waiting for curtains, and the tangle of hanging clothes flopped over a chair. She squinched her eyes shut, then forced them wide open in an effort to stay awake. "I don't think so. Thanks though."

He left the room, but her next words made him pause halfway across the loft. "Why are there two cribs in Jade's room?" She leaned against the doorway.

"Oh, that. I'd forgotten." He suddenly looked tired. "When Jade and I moved here, my G-mom helped me set it all up. At that time, we thought I might be adopting Jade's younger sibling. I haven't had the heart to take it down."

Kiera nodded, catching the sadness behind his words.

"Goodnight."

Kiera gave a little wave and immediately wished

she could think of something more to say. She turned back into her room instead, shutting the door behind her. She felt like crying when she looked at the boxes. Only five left to unpack, but five too many. Sitting down on the sheetless bed and opening her purse, she found the device while she was looking for her leftover Mandie's chocolate and clicked the message app on a whim.

> Hi Mom!
> Do you have time for a voice call? I'm too tired to sleep, and there's too much to do before tomorrow.

She broke off another square of chocolate and let it melt on her tongue, waking her up a little more.

Mom's message blinked up on the screen.

> Sure honey, I can call. You okay?

Kiera hurried to send a reply, typos and all.

> Too tired to type. Talking better. Have to be quiet for Jade tho.

She set the device on her desk and waited for Mom to call. Which box had pajamas in it again? She checked the labels and kicked herself for labeling them all "Dresser". Whatever. She would change into them when she found them. More reasons to unpack tonight. She ripped back the tape of the first box with Mandie's-induced bravery.

The device announced Mom was calling, and she hurried to accept it.

"Hi, Kiera! How are you, honey?"

Her insides melted and she felt like crying from relief. Moving to a new house wasn't so bad; it was leaving her old home that put an ache in her heart. She wiped her eyes and suddenly realized she hadn't said any of this aloud.

"I'm doing all right. I'm homesick already." She laughed at herself in an effort to assure Mom she was really okay.

"We miss you too, dear."

Kiera yawned. "Brennan and I lugged everything upstairs, and I'm pretty far through unpacking. Jade's already been in bed for a few hours. She fell asleep on the way over. It was pretty cute."

Mom chuckled. "Oh, that's sweet! You're going to have to send me pictures of your room when you're done unpacking."

"You wouldn't want to see it right now, that's for sure," Kiera said, accidentally spilling crafting supplies across the floor. She sat down to scrape beads back into their container. "I'll send some soon though. I probably won't be done with the niceties until Monday, but I'm hoping to have all my clothes in order tonight so I can actually find things in the morning."

"I put a couple of my headcoverings in your purse just in case you and Brennan decide that's something you want to do."

Kiera froze and squeezed her thumb. "Thank you."

"How is it going with Brennan, dear?"

She sighed. "All right, I guess. He told me nothing needs to change between us, but it's already so different. I balk at talking to him, because I'm afraid of being flirty or losing his friendship." She yawned. "The same old trouble with guys, except I'm married to this one."

Finally! She'd found pajamas. She paused to pull a nightgown over her head. "He's been so good to me that I just want to do exactly what would be right for him."

"I get your thinking; just make sure it's not pride or perfectionism. And if I know Brennan, he won't take it as flirting if you are just plain friendly. Try to treat him exactly the way you did on your birthday when you opened the door wearing that hat."

They laughed together, and Kiera interjected, "Destiny almost killed me."

"No really," Mom went on, "treat him like you would Aric. Let him be your friend but don't ask for anything more."

Kiera sat down in front of the device and rested her chin in her hands. "'Kay. Thanks, Mom."

"Anytime, dear. Call me whenever you like. I should probably be going now, but I look forward to seeing you tomorrow."

Kiera yawned again. "Yeah, I should probably go too."

"Goodnight, Kiera."

"Goodnight, Mommy."

She stumbled around the room awhile longer after the call had ended, trying to forget that it was eleven at night and she hadn't slept normally in two days. All the boxes were broken down and things were mostly in order when she slid between her stiff sheets to go to sleep.

She turned out her lamp and stared at the pitch-black ceiling. Her fingers found her ring and traced the circle it made around her finger. Should she take it off, or did married women wear their rings at all times?

Her mind drifted to church the next day. What was Thorne going to preach about? She made a mental note to return a book to Destiny and sat bolt upright, wide awake. Praying for the right words to say, Kiera opened the device and started typing a new message.

Hi Tiny!
Why am I up this late? I was about to ask why are you, but the device says you're not on. I guess you'll find this in the morning, hopefully before church. It's kinda important. I know we didn't talk yesterday, but I have some big news for you. I married Brennan Stewart.

I feel horrible about not telling you sooner because we've always promised each other to be bridesmaids and everything, but it's not like that, and it all happened so fast. It's not what you think. Thursday night Brennan approached my parents with the idea of us getting married so I wouldn't get drafted. You know I've always liked Brennan, but he's never noticed me. This is entirely just so I won't get drafted.

In some ways, this feels pretty weird to me, but he wants what is best for me, and that really is the true definition of love, isn't it? Pray for us, girly.

I'm lonely for popcorn wars and home.

Fist bumps and firecrackers, Kiera

CHAPTER TEN
Church

Kiera was cracking eggs when Brennan stumbled into the kitchen and straight toward the coffeepot. She threw another eggshell into the compost bin and began to whisk the bowl of egg yolks. Her damp hair threatened to trail forward into the bowl, but she pushed it back over her shoulders and snuck a glance at him. Time to follow Mom's advice.

"Good morning!" she said brightly, pouring the eggs into a sizzling frying pan.

Brennan turned away from adding cream to his cup. His eyes drooped with traces of sleep, but he managed a tired smile. "You're up early. Do you want some?" He gestured with his mug.

"No, thanks. I don't like how it tastes." She wrinkled up her nose and grinned apologetically. "It's gonna take me a few to get breakfast on the table, if you want to switch the order of getting ready and eating."

He downed his coffee and nodded, eyes beginning to look more awake. "Sounds good to me. Smells good too," he replied as he left the kitchen.

Kiera shook her head. She had managed to avoid asking about headcovering, but she couldn't continue all morning. Headcovering would be a big, public reminder to everyone that they were married, and the personal element made her feel embarrassed all over.

Everyone might as well get used to it. Including Kiera herself. She sighed and continued arguing with herself as she cut up fruit into a bowl. Setting the food on the table, she covered the eggs and returned to the kitchen for plates.

Satisfied that everything was ready, she hurried upstairs to get Jade. Slowly opening the door to the nursery, she walked across the soft candy-striped rug and raised the curtain to fill the room with morning light. Jade rolled over and rubbed her eyes before stumbling to her feet with the help of the crib side.

"Good morning, big girl!" Kiera said, her face breaking into a smile.

"Hi." Jade smiled sleepily and reached up to be lifted out.

"Today's church, so we need to get you dressed real quick before breakfast," Kiera explained, giving her a good-morning squeeze and setting her down. She rolled back the closet door and took down two church dresses. "Which one do you want?"

Jade took her thumb out of her mouth long

enough to point at the pink dress with a toile skirt. Kiera helped her into the dress and buttoned up the back. A diaper change and curly pigtails later, they were walking hand in hand down the stairs. Kiera glanced at the kitchen clock and knew Brennan would be joining them soon. She would have to ask him her question eventually.

She had just buckled Jade into her highchair and sat in the chair next to her when Brennan came down the stairs.

Jade clapped. "Yay, Daddy!"

"Yay, Jade!" Brennan clapped, and they all shared a laugh that helped ease the tension as they prayed together and served out breakfast.

"I have a lot a lot of apples?" Jade asked, doing a grabbing gesture at the fruit.

Kiera turned to Brennan with a questioning look.

"Go ahead and answer her however you think best," he responded.

She nodded slightly and turned to Jade. "After you eat your eggs, you can have 'a lot a lot' of apples."

Jade began obediently cramming eggs into her mouth and was soon ready for the first of many apples.

Kiera looked at Brennan and twisted her ring in her lap. "I—I was wondering what you thought about headcoverings."

He cocked his head and ran his fingers through his damp hair. No wonder it was always so unruly—he never gave it a chance to dry flat. "What did your family do?"

That one word *did* made her sigh inside. "Mom covers her head as their understanding of the passage in First Peter. They interpret it as applying to married women during the church meeting, so I wasn't required to practice it although I know some families ask their daughters to."

Brennan set down his fork and rested his elbows on the edge of the table. "And what were you planning to do before…" he trailed off, looking at her intently.

Kiera squeezed her thumb in the folds of her skirt. "Whatever my husband preferred since it is a symbol of submission." She gave a little smile.

"I've always admired your mom and the other women who cover their heads. Not because they do it, but because it seems to be a natural outworking of their relationship with their husband."

She gave Jade another apple and turned back to him, surprised he had noticed.

"Thank you for asking me. It means a lot that you did." He smiled. "If you are willing, I think I would like it," he finished, looking at her steadily.

She met his gaze and nodded easily.

Kiera shut her bedroom door and changed into a dressier shirt, shaking the apron-induced wrinkles out of her lace skirt. Running a brush through her hair, she hurried to apply her makeup, keeping one eye on the clock. She yanked a bureau drawer open and rummaged through for the headcoverings Mom had given her. Gray and brown scarves. She would need a fuller palette later, but this was a good start.

Kiera chose the charcoal-gray one and set to work. She had never paid much attention to how Mom had tied hers, but it couldn't be too hard. Chances were Brennan didn't know how it was supposed to look either, so she wouldn't gain any advice from that source. She pulled up a few videos on the device and tried to follow the instructions backward and behind her head.

It was still in her thoughts as a small worry when she led Jade up the church steps. Brennan hung back so they would enter at the same time. She gave him a grateful look and steeled herself for the noisy, unwelcoming atmosphere of the lobby. A group of teenage girls nearby laughed loudly, and a tiny child ran by with his mother chasing after him.

"Oh, Kiera! Beautiful scarf." The woman paused to talk, completely losing sight of her child. "Care to share the happy news?"

Kiera smiled slightly. "Brennan Stewart and I were married yesterday."

A smile plastered itself on the woman's face. "Well, congratulations!" She scanned the crowd and took off after her child, adding to herself with a smirk, "Like I didn't see that coming."

Kiera stared after her for a moment, swallowing the questions that rose in her mind. Mom and Dad flashed her a smile across the room, and she answered with a wave. She reached up absently to feel her headcovering and was surprised by a backward hug.

"Destiny, let go so I can turn around and give you a proper hug," she laughed.

Destiny complied. "You look so cute in that, girl," she said, reaching up to tweak her scarf. "But why didn't you tell me sooner? I would have rushed down to your house and been a bridesmaid right then and there."

Kiera's heart sank at the hurt look on her friend's face. "I...um, it was decided very last minute, and then, when it did happen, I was so busy and worried and...I'm sorry."

"Yeah, it's okay." Destiny smiled weakly. "Life doesn't always turn out the way we plan it, does it?"

Kiera shook her head slightly.

"Hey, I think church might be starting without us. I'd better go sit down. I don't want to miss a word Thorne says," Destiny said, giving a little wave and hustling exaggeratedly into the sanctuary in her high heels.

Kiera followed her and stopped just inside the door. As she watched Destiny turn away to sit with her family, Kent caught her eye, frightening her with the dark flash of anger she found there. She turned away and scanned the other rows to find Brennan. He waved at her, and she started toward him, sliding into the pew to sit on the other side of Jade. Somehow with him blocking her from the aisle she felt safe but still shaken. Why was Kent angry with her?

She handed Brennan his Bible and opened her own. Thorne began the service in prayer, and she took a deep breath, forcing herself to concentrate. Brennan's pen scratched away next to her, and someone in the congregation coughed.

Jade grew sleepy and laid her head down on Kiera's lap. She stroked the loose pigtails, then realized with a start how silent the congregation had become. There were no amens, no coughs, no nods or head shaking, nothing. She sat up, alert now, and focused on Thorne's words.

"When we come to Christ, we surrender to Him as Savior and Lord. His being our Lord starts here on earth just like His being our Savior does. From the moment we come to Him, we surrender to Him daily. We live as His. In every area of life, He is the one Who gets the say in how we live as His precious, set-apart people."

Someone murmured from the back in answer.

Brennan's pen grew silent and he turned to her, speaking in an undertone, "Kiera, what's wrong?"

"They don't agree with him. Even on something as basic as this." She looked away. "None of them. They aren't even listening." Her words trailed off and her shoulders sank.

"Someone is. Look." He nodded his head toward the Moores' row where Aric sat drinking the words in. "God is still working."

CHAPTER ELEVEN
Mommy

Kiera yawned and stretched as she entered the kitchen. Her to-do list was short, but the main task would take all day to complete: getting familiar with the kitchen and putting together a meal plan. She had been busy unpacking all morning, and the few hours after church the day before had been spent in awkward silence as they caught up on correspondence or read, or at least Brennan did.

Twisting her hair, she pinned it up and tied an apron on over her clothes. It was time to get down to business if she wanted to finish before Jade's nap ended. She reached for the first drawer and paused with her hand on the knob.

"Silverware?" she guessed aloud, smiling ruefully when she saw a stack of dish towels. This was going to take forever. Thank goodness the cabinets had glass fronts.

The kitchen was small and the drawers organized

logically enough that after a few more rounds of this game she could find everything. At least on the second try. Brennan's "G-mom" had certainly known what she was doing when she set it up. She half-wondered if Brennan had changed a thing.

Grabbing the pad of paper she had stuck in her apron pocket, Kiera opened the refrigerator door and knelt in front of it.

"Two pounds of beef, apples, three heads of lettuce…" She tucked her hair behind her ears and jotted down notes. Later she would arrange it into a menu that would last them until next Saturday when Brennan could run errands again. She stood up and shut the doors.

There wasn't much in the freezer except frozen meat, but she made sure to take stock of all that as well. This was when Proverbs 31 rubber met the road, and the words "she looks well to the ways of her household" came to mind.

Jade called from upstairs, and Kiera smiled. The house had been so quiet she had been talking to herself and even contemplating turning on music. Stuffing her paper and pencil into her pocket, she hurried to go get her little girl.

"Hi, little friend!" she exclaimed, reaching for Jade.

Jade put her arms around Kiera's neck as she lifted her out of the crib.

"Mommy has been looking at the food. Do you want to help her?" She felt a little guilty referring to herself by that name. It felt wrong somehow.

"Uh…yesh," Jade replied after a moment of thought. Her pigtails from the morning had shaken out during her nap, and her hair stuck up in a wild mass of sweaty curls.

Kiera laughed and kissed her mane. "Then let's get to work."

The refrigerator and freezer were both inventoried, but Kiera guessed they kept most of the food in the pantry. She wandered into the muggy garage and found the pantry tucked in one corner.

"Are these p-pota-tatoes?" Jade asked, pointing at the small bin piled high with them.

"Yes, and it looks like there are…" she began counting but Jade stopped her.

"I do it?" she asked.

Kiera smiled. "Sure, but I'll help you."

They had soon counted all one hundred and four potatoes, sixty seventy yams, and eight carrots. She almost giggled at the wild numbers Jade came up with, but she did her best to straighten her out and write down the real answers. She even tried to point out the different colors, figuring that preschool had to start sometime, but Jade was too distracted to remember very long which ones were which. They would have to stick to dolls' names for now.

Kiera picked up her little girl and caught her breath. "Well, dearie, I think that's everything. Before Mommy starts on the menu planning, let's take a break and have a snack. Deal?" There it was. Mommy again. It just slipped out.

"Yay, snack!" Chubby hands clapped together.

Kiera laughed again. She loved this time with her little friend. Moments later they were sitting in dining chairs munching on carrots and apple slices and making funny faces at each other.

Someone needed to know about the cuteness.

She flipped open the device and said to Jade, "Let's call Uncle Thorny."

"Clawk?"

"No, not Grandpa." She had better start referring to everyone as Jade's relatives. It would help her to get used to the change as well. She scanned the face calling app and quickly realized he wasn't on. Probably busy preparing his Easter sermon.

"On second thought, let's message him."

"I type?"

"Please?"

"I type, pleash?"

Kiera giggled at her pronunciation and settled her on her lap in answer. Jade pounded out a message.

aerhelkajhKJRQal;rkje;lwr;j.

"Good job. Now it's Mommy's turn. Can you go get a dolly?"

Jade slid off her lap, eager to do the errand.

Heya, Thorny.
Hope you enjoyed that message from Jade.

She's been so cute today that I had to tell someone. She counts everything in impossibly large numbers, but she's eager to learn. Preschool will be no problem.

Yikes, it's weird to think of preschool! I've been referring to myself as 'Mommy' all day, which is odd but it helps me somehow. Oh, and she also learned to say device…sort of. It came out more as "did-eyes" or something weird. ;)

She hasn't named you yet, but we'll work on that. I'll make sure it's horrid enough. I miss you, and I can't wait to hear the Easter sermon you are undoubtedly working on. Or are you rallying with Jessica?
Your sister chronically, Kiera

She sent the message and stood up. Where was Jade? The distractible toddler had settled in a corner with a pile of dolls, and she decided to fit in a few breakfast and snack dishes. The dishes piled up first in the sink, then on the counter as she hummed a tune to keep her loneliness at arm's length.

Kiera hung up her dish towel and returned to the sink to give it a final cleaning, then gasped as she caught her ring from nearly going down the drain. Married women took them off when they did dishes. Why couldn't she remember?

That's when she really cried.

❧

Her menu was perfect. It had taken two days to finish, but it was worth it. At first she had thought it best to make it on the device, but an old-fashioned fit had come upon her, and she decided to scrawl it out on paper.

Jade lay on her stomach nearby drawing squiggles in the margins of the calendar and declaring them to be dollies, as usual.

Kiera studied the menu again. An offhand comment Brennan had made last night brought a whole new area of meal planning to mind. He bought his meals at work! How in the world did he find anything nutritionally okay? How much money did he spend on it a year? She knew it had always been his only option.

She would cook ahead for him. She had the time, and since she was his helper it was partly her business to care for his health and finances.

She shook her head. That morning had marked the beginning of their third day of "marriage", and still they were barely talking. It was silly of them to act this way since both were immediately relieved when the ice was broken. Mentally running through a list of "safe" conversations or activities they could do together, her mind came up blank.

"Mommy, I drawing the picture!"

Her heart squeezed. It was one thing to call herself Mommy, and another to hear her daughter say it.

"It looks beautiful! What is it?" she asked, leaning over to kiss her on the head and have a closer look.

"Uh…dinner!"

Kiera glanced at the device clock. Time to test her shiny new meal plan.

"Okay, time to put away the coloring stuff and work on dinner," she said, reaching for a few art pencils to put them in their zippered pouch.

"I not done."

"Mommy says it's time to be done."

"No!" She pulled the pouch away and took the pencils out.

"Jade."

"I draaaawing."

Kiera stood and picked the toddler up, letting the art pencils fall to the floor in a clatter. She turned to go upstairs, shutting the device as she went by. Tears began to flood her eyes as she realized what this would do to her schedule. So much for dinner on time.

As she climbed the stairs with Jade tucked under her arm like an oversized cloth doll, she began to laugh. Here she was preparing to deal with a willful toddler while complaining in her own heart. She walked into Jade's room and set her in one of the white cribs, then sat with her back against the other to calm down. Mom had always modeled having a right heart before correcting a child.

She ignored Jade's complaining and shut her eyes to still her heart and pray. "I'm sorry, Lord. I had so many big plans for today of how to love my new family by serving them. I wanted to cook ahead for Brennan to bless him and to feel useful to his life. I was about to lose sight of one of the most important ways You've called me to love Jade. Please forgive me and help me to discipline her in a way that honors You."

Kiera opened her eyes and looked around the room at the soft pink walls, the white changing table under the sunny window, and the fuzzy sheep-like rug under her feet. She stroked the plush carpet for a moment before looking up at the angry red toddler face glaring at her.

"Jade, it's time to stop crying," she said patiently.

"No!" Jade shook her head and her wild hair spun around her.

Kiera gave the toddler a light spank. Jade looked surprised and rubbed the spot. She stopped crying for a moment.

"Jade, it's time to be sweet. Say 'yes, Mommy'."

"No!"

Another spank. Kiera hated doing it.

"Say 'yes, Mommy'."

"Yesh, Mommy."

"Good girl, Jade!" She let out a sigh of relief and hugged the toddler.

"Dinner, now?" Jade asked.

She smiled. "Let's go get it ready."

CHAPTER TWELVE
Gray Fabric

Kiera sat at the kitchen table sipping a cup of tea and reading a cheerful message from Mom. Jade had been tucked into bed long ago, and she relished the quiet evening alone. It wasn't quite alone since Brennan was reading on the couch across the room, but he only stirred from his book to stand his hair all on end or change position.

She smiled at his relaxed expression and regretted needing to interrupt him. Glancing down at the device, she cleared her throat.

He looked up. "Need something?"

"I know it's really late notice, but Mom offered to take me fabric shopping tomorrow. I thought it might be good to get Jade's wardrobe ready for spring. Do you think that's a possibility?" She looked away. "She'd pick me up. It's okay if not."

"No, it's good you thought of it. I'm not in touch with those sorts of things." He smiled sheepishly and sat up further. "How much do you need?"

He named an amount, and she gulped in surprise. "That's more than enough."

"Well, you're going to need things too, right?"

She nodded.

"I'll get it to you tomorrow when I come home from work. Deal?"

"Thank you."

Kiera quickly wrote a reply to Mom, then drafted a list of items she knew both she and Jade would need. She could already think of a few things that were wearing thin.

"Did I ever loan you the second book?"

She startled. Brennan was speaking.

"The one you returned on your birthday. I said there were seven more. I'm on the…" he flipped the book over to look at the spine, "third book."

"No, you didn't."

"I'm sorry I forgot. Things have been a little different." He shrugged and grinned apologetically. "I'll grab it, if you'd like to borrow it."

Kiera studied him for a moment and was struck by his friendliness. She gave a small smile. "I'd love to."

Brennan set his book down and disappeared upstairs. Kiera closed the device and rinsed out her empty mug. Setting it in the bottom of the sink, she entered the living room and scrunched herself up on the couch opposite the dog-eared book.

"Here we are." Brennan held the battered copy out

to her. "Don't read chapter twelve while it's dark out."

She laughed. "A little creepy?"

"Well, maybe it was that I was all alone while I read it, but yeah." He flopped down on the couch and opened his book.

Kiera grinned to herself. Now she could join in on the evening reading sessions.

Kiera threw her hair into a loose side braid and pulled on her knee socks. She checked her face in the mirror and was relieved to find that her makeup was still mostly intact from the morning's application. Hearing footsteps on the stairs, she slid open her closet door and reached for a sweater but grabbed a light coat instead. It was still barely spring, and rain could be hiding around any corner.

She opened her door to see Brennan coming up the stairs with Jade under one arm like a sack of potatoes. Words froze inside her as he looked at her outfit and reached into his pocket for the finances he had promised. Treat him like Aric or the book reading buddy he was.

Kiera gestured to Jade. "Is she in trouble or stinky?"

That prompted a grin. "Stinky. We're gonna fix that though, eh, Princess?"

"Princess, eh?" She smiled at him and took the card he held out.

"Every little girl needs a nickname. Hey, have fun with your mom."

"Thank you."

He moved past her into the nursery, and she hurried downstairs to the tune of the doorbell. Seconds later she was enveloped in one of Mom's famous hugs.

"I've missed you so much, Mom," Kiera whispered.

"I've missed you too, honey. We have a lot of catching up to do."

The drizzly rain Kiera had inwardly predicted was already streaking the car windows as they pulled out of the driveway.

"Would you check my device for the forecast, please?" Mom handed her the familiar machine she had done years of schoolwork on.

She scrolled through the apps. "No radiation."

"Phew, I am not dressed for it."

Mom punched in a few coordinates, and the car shifted itself into the right lane. They sat together in companionable silence as they were navigated through several neighborhoods and crowded streets before the fabric warehouse loomed up in front of them. They unbuckled their seat belts and dodged puddles as they walked through the parking lot. Kiera was keenly aware of Brennan's card in her purse, and she clutched it a little tighter.

"It was awkward asking him for finances," were

her first words a few minutes later as they chose a cart.

"Why?" Mom asked, studying the map on her phone for a moment, then setting off in a random direction in the store.

"I don't know. I guess it's because I feel so much in his debt. I only asked for enough for Jade, and he gave me enough for both of us and more." She hurried to catch up with her.

"That's very generous of him. And since he had a sister, he was probably guessing you would want something special for Easter."

Kiera smiled, remembering his advice to enjoy herself.

"Can you tell me more about Shannon?" she asked later on, running her fingers across several bolts of denim. "Brennan hasn't said much about her yet."

Mom sighed, and tears rose in her eyes. "I won't tell you any more than what he's willing to tell people, but they both had a very hard childhood. He responded to God; she did not. It grieves him very much."

A sick feeling was forming in the pit of Kiera's stomach. No wonder he never spoke of her.

"Shannon gave birth to Jade, and he quit the last semester of college to get a job so he could adopt her. Later that year, Shannon joined the military. He didn't even get to say goodbye."

Kiera covered her hands with her face. She had never heard the whole story. No wonder he valued

Thorne's friendship so much. Mom drew her arms around her.

She wiped her eyes and looked at the stack of bolts in her cart and the few in Mom's. Even with the Easter dresses, she would still have money left over.

"Are you ready to go get it cut?" Mom asked.

Kiera hesitated for a moment. "I need to get one more thing."

She would make him a shirt. Dark gray. It would postpone her goal of cooking ahead, but she didn't care. Such a man deserved such a gift.

Kiera spread out the fabrics on the kitchen table and played with a stray thread. Three dresses for Jade, two skirts for herself—one formal and the other for every day, as well as some neutral blouses. The teal bolt of fabric waited nearby to be made into Easter dresses.

The silky fabric called to her, but she set it aside with a sigh and started on one of Jade's everyday dresses. The scissors squeaked as they sliced through the pink polka-dot fabric. Crisp cuts and straight edges. Shining pins piercing through layers of fabric.

Kiera grinned with delight as the tiny dress began to take shape. It was the first thing she had ever made for Jade, besides a red beret last Christmas. She hummed to herself as she sewed, the whir of the machine as loud as an old manual car.

Time slipped away like fabric through her fingers, and one dress and no dinner was finished when Brennan arrived.

"Daddy, yook! I has dress!" Jade took it off the table and held it up for him to see.

Kiera watched in amusement as they examined the dress while she extricated herself from the sewing machine cord and began cleaning up. It was worth a later dinner to see Jade's joy.

"It looks good," Brennan commented, taking it from her to examine it. He looked up at Kiera. "You did a good job; I barely knew it was homemade."

"Thank you." She smiled with pleasure at his words.

"Is this the rest of your fabric? I never saw what you brought home." He came over to look at the stack she was getting ready to put away.

Kiera was immediately glad the gray fabric was hidden in her room. "You gave me enough that I was able to spend some on fabric for Easter dresses," she said, showing him the teal bolt. "Both Jade and I are looking forward to them."

"That makes three of us then. Can I take your machine upstairs for you?"

Kiera twisted her ring and found the words to say yes. A part of her had hoped Brennan would like her new dress, but another was slightly embarrassed that he noticed her appearance. Maybe she should put in a little more effort beyond just brushing her hair.

After a day or so more of trying to be practical, Kiera had finished Jade's clothes and convinced herself that the remaining four days until Easter should really be spent on the dresses. She shook with excitement and nervousness when she first cut into the silky blue cloth. At least this time she had a real pattern.

Work on Brennan's shirt was tucked into moments when he was gone or asleep. She cut it out early Saturday morning but hid it away during the day and finished hemming her dress instead. It had turned out better than she could have hoped, and she hung it up on the outside of her closet door where she could brush her fingers along it and make it swing whenever she walked by.

Brennan seemed to have no intention of going anywhere all day, and she kept herself from accidentally spoiling the surprise by making a pan of celebratory cinnamon rolls and reading the suggested passage for Holy Week.

Finally when she was about to take the machine up to her room where she could sew in secret, he yawned and shut his book.

"Six o'clock comes early. I think I'll go upstairs now."

She fiddled with a piece of thread to make herself look busy and nodded. "I have a little bit more to do, but I'll try to be quiet down here."

He smiled. "Well, goodnight then."

"Goodnight." Was this the first time she had said it?

CHAPTER THIRTEEN
Easter Sunday

Kiera sat bolt upright in bed, slapping her hand against her forehead. She had left the gray shirt on the ironing board downstairs. She had barely been able to drag herself to bed, much less clean up the night before. Rushing down the stairs, she snatched it up, slid the cinnamon rolls in the oven to warm, and ran back to her room before she got caught, curlers and all.

Giggling to herself at the absurdity of it all, she spread the shirt out on her bed to inspect it once more. Every stitch was perfect. Sure, she had had to put one sleeve on three times and change the bobbin twice that many, but this was her gift to the man who had given her so much. She tucked a hanger into the buttoned collar and snuck to the bathroom to hang it up where Brennan would find it.

Her alarm finally went off, and she rummaged through her closet to grab something comfortable to wear until she changed into her dress. Untwisting the curlers from her hair, she piled them on her desk and applied her makeup. A repetitive banging on the other side of the wall alerted her that Jade was awake, and soon after, the shower started, signaling her that Brennan was also up.

Shaking out her curls, she pinned them into a loose bun, still adjusting the strands around her face as she opened Jade's door.

"Good morning, Jade!"

"Mommy, I has cinnamon rolls, pleash?"

She laughed. "After we get you ready, okay?"

"I has dress?"

"Yes, you are going to finally get to wear your dress."

Moments later, Jade was spinning around the room, giggling at the way her dress stood out from her.

"Do you like it?"

More giggles answered.

"Now we are going to take you to Mommy's room to do your hair."

She settled Jade down on the chair in front of the mirror and softly brushed her curls until they shone. Pulling Jade's hair into her usual pigtails, she added a sparkly clip and pronounced it finished.

"Okay, now I need you to sit on my bed while I change into *my* princess dress."

Kiera set her in the middle of the bed and ducked into the closet. She could hear the little girl singing a song about dresses and smiled to herself over the words.

Downstairs, Kiera strapped Jade into her highchair, then covered her own dress with an old apron, feeling the smooth fabric beneath her fingers. It had turned out perfectly. One look at Brennan told Kiera he hadn't chosen to wear the shirt, and disappointment blew the morning sunshine away. She tried to ignore it, but it nearly brought her to tears as they prayed together and made chitchat about the day. She had been more excited about his gift than the silky teal dresses.

She was just putting on her own pumps and buttoning Jade's sweater when Brennan came down the stairs, swinging the hanger in one hand.

"Was this supposed to come with us?"

She swallowed. "Only if you wanted to wear it."

He stared at her blankly. "Wait, this is for me?"

She nodded and squeezed her thumb, crumpling the folds of her skirt.

"And here I was envying Thorne." He grinned at the shirt. "Can you wait a moment in the car while I change out of these old rags?"

Kiera twisted her ring and took Jade's hand. The smile she gave him lit her whole face. "We can wait."

The church building was full to bursting, and people were still arriving. Kiera hugged Jade close to herself and tried not to let the obnoxious sounds of the crowd get to her. She couldn't even find Destiny in the sea of faces. Brennan led them into the sanctuary where they claimed two rows.

"You said all your brothers were coming, right?" Brennan looked up and down the rows. "Think this will be enough?"

"Should be fine." She shrugged.

Mom and Dad soon joined them with Ian, Rachel, and their four little children trailing behind. There were hugs all around before they squeezed into the pew, and Brennan and Kiera sat down behind them with Jade in between them.

"Is this seat taken?" One of the deacons' wives approached the end of the row.

"I'm so sorry, but I think it is," Mom said politely and suggested an empty spot a few rows up.

Kiera waited for her response and breathed a sigh of relief when none came. The woman always intimidated her.

"All the family here, I see."

Mom smiled. "Jordan and Niyanna are on their way. Is your son coming?"

She shook her head regretfully. "Too busy with wedding planning, you know?"

Kiera whispered to Brennan, "Thorne is officiating his and Shelby's wedding next week."

"Busy man," he replied.

"You all had a wedding in the family recently as

well, I see," the deacon's wife continued, looking at Kiera.

"Yes, just recently," Mom replied, smiling at Kiera.

The woman walked away, and soon Jordan and Niyanna arrived, herding their children into the pew. Kiera grinned at Niyanna in greeting, and her little niece Madelyn immediately planted herself next to Kiera. In only a few minutes, she was fast friends with Jade and her coloring supplies. Mom and the others immediately launched into a discussion of potty training.

"Kiera, I love your dress. Did you make it?" Niyanna asked, pushing the thick black curls back from her forehead. She was always interested in fabrics and the art of fashion.

Kiera nodded happily in reply.

"Jade's too, and Brennan's shirt," Mom added proudly.

"I was hoping to take pictures of everyone when we go to Dad and Mom's for dinner, but now I definitely have to," Niyanna decided.

Kiera darted a glance at Brennan. Family pictures! Niyanna's photographer sensibilities wouldn't understand unless it was explained.

"It would be so sweet to have a picture of all the little girls together, especially since Jade and Madelyn look like twins," Rachel agreed quietly. Her shiny brown hair was pulled back from her face in a twist, and she looked at her family with gentle pride.

Kiera turned to Brennan with a silent question.

"Just as long as I get a picture of me tackling Thorne, I'm game."

Everyone laughed, and Kiera relaxed enough to notice that the sanctuary was filling up and Thorne had taken his place in the front row. Joy surged through her as she joined her family in standing to sing familiar Easter hymns, and she winked at Jordan when his rich bass came in.

Brennan held Jade in one arm, and Kiera held Madelyn in the other. Between them they held the hymn book, and she made goofy faces over it at the nephew resting his head on Ian's shoulder. By the time Thorne opened his Bible to Galatians 2 and began his sermon, her niece was asleep in her arms and beginning to feel very heavy.

"Why don't you lay her down on the pew? We've still got a bit of room left in this sardine can," Brennan suggested, and she willingly took him up on the offer.

"A little bit of room" meant Jade had to sit on his lap; and Kiera realized that in the three weeks since he had given her the ring, this was the first time they had sat together. His gray sleeve brushed her arm as he opened his Bible, and she looked at him so apparently at home and comfortable next to her.

"'I have been crucified with Christ...'" Thorne was reading aloud, "'it is no longer I who live, but Christ lives in me; and the life which I now live in the flesh I live by faith in the Son of God, who loved me and gave Himself for me.' Our sin is dead, and now we are alive in Christ. But how are we living? A life of faith or of dead works?"

Kiera yawned. It had taken Niyanna a characteristically long time to edit the family pictures to her liking and get them sent out to everyone, but they all agreed it was worth the wait. Earlier that day Mom had dropped by for a visit, and Kiera and Jade had looked through them to help her choose which ones to print. But something inside her wanted to savor them, and now Kiera was up late scrolling through them again.

Jordan had gained possession of the camera first since Niyanna had wanted "sister" pictures. Even quiet Rachel had gotten into the mood, and a few delightfully silly pictures had resulted. Kiera paged through shots of the little kids, of the "brothers" tackling each other, and of Mom and Dad posing sweetly together. Then there was a strictly sibling picture, and Kiera grinned at the protective way her tall brothers stood around her.

She bit her lip as she raced through pictures of Ian and Rachel smiling with their little flock and proudly pointing out the baby to come. Jordan and Niyanna were enthusiastic and adorable. As opposite in looks as two people could be with his straight, light-brown hair and her luxurious black curls; but one in spirit, especially the spirit of goofiness.

She slowed down when she reached the pictures of her "family" looking sharp in the clothes she had sewn for them. Jade being "flown" by her daddy on one side and Kiera on the other. They were laughing together like old friends, and her heart warmed at the giggle on the toddler's face.

She hadn't realized how comfortable it had become between her and Brennan until she looked at these pictures and the days following them. Just weeks ago, she had been too shy to ask about head covering, and now they flopped on opposite ends of the couch and fought over fan theories in the series they shared. Kiera smiled slightly at the thought.

She turned off the device and sat down on her bed to read a few verses before turning out the light and burrowing down deep into the covers. The slight headache that had bothered her all day seemed to intensify into a drumming inside her head.

She was just falling asleep when she heard crying on the other side of the wall. She groaned. It grew louder. Sitting up, she rubbed her eyes and grabbed her robe before slipping out into the hall to check on Jade.

"Jade, it's okay. Mommy's here." She felt for the light switch in the dark and turned it on to find Jade blinking and rubbing tears from her eyes.

"I icky."

Kiera came closer. The poor baby had lost her

dinner all over the crib and her sleeper.

"Aw, poor princess! We'll get you cleaned up in a second." She darted to the bathroom for a towel and came back just in time to catch it happening again.

Jade was crying feverishly, and it was all she could do to get her out of the crib.

"Shhh, it's okay. You're gonna be okay. Let Mommy fix it." She crooned to the toddler as she took off the dirty sleeper and wrapped her in the last clean towel.

Wadding up the sleeper and the dirty towel, she set them aside and sat on the floor, melting Jade into her lap and rocking her gently. The toddler began crying again, and she dove for the towel. Moments later, Brennan blinked in the doorway, wearing a sweat-stained white T-shirt and an exhausted but worried expression.

"Kiera, what's wrong?"

"Jade's vomiting."

"What do you need?"

"More towels and the supplements from the refrigerator door? After that, I'll need clean sheets, but that's a long way off."

He disappeared, and she went back to stroking Jade's limp hair off her forehead. She leaned against the other crib and briefly wondered why she had asked for sheets instead of just using the extra crib. It was almost as if it permanently belonged to another child.

Brennan appeared, a little more awake this time,

and set the pile of towels down, then handed her the jar of ginger tincture.

"Thanks," she said as she filled the oral syringe and forced it between Jade's lips.

Jade squirmed and whimpered.

"Jade, it's okay. This will make you not icky."

The toddler fought harder, and Brennan sat down cross-legged on the floor. "Hold her still, and I'll give it to her."

Kiera breathed a sigh of relief when the supplement was finally administered, and Jade lay back against her sleepily.

"Do you want this put away?" Brennan asked, holding up the jar of tincture.

"I'll need it again soon, so go ahead and set it on the bureau." Feeling slightly more certain that Jade wasn't going to vomit again anytime soon, she stood up and selected a new sleeper to dress her in.

"Anything else?"

"Thanks for asking, but I think we'll be all right now if you want to catch some more sleep before work tomorrow."

He nodded sleepily and disappeared across the loft. Kiera set Jade in the middle of the floor and stripped the sheets off the crib. It was the work of a few minutes to replace them with new sheets, carry everything down to the laundry room, and run back up the stairs to give Jade another dosage of tincture. She was nearly asleep this time, making it much easier, and

Kiera tucked her into her crib with an extra blanket.

Standing at the doorway to her own room, nervousness seized her, and on impulse she grabbed her blanket and pillow and returned to Jade's room. She was tired enough to sleep on the floor.

CHAPTER FOURTEEN
Not of the World

"Somebody feels better than their mommy today," Kiera murmured as she stumbled down the stairs after the toddler.

She had forgotten to bring her alarm clock to the impromptu sleepover and guessed the time was somewhere between breakfast and lunch. Jade climbed the side of her highchair and plopped down in the seat.

Kiera clapped a hand to her aching forehead. "Oh, right. Food. I don't want any, but I'll grab you some." She leaned over to open the refrigerator, and the room spun around her.

It was all she could do to stay upright as she peeled a hard-boiled egg and rinsed some grapes to set out on Jade's highchair tray. Stumbling back upstairs, she changed into a comfortable skirt and oversized T-shirt.

Kiera scraped together a random pile of toys next to the couch. With Jade safely occupied, she sank into the cushions with the third book in Brennan's series. Her eyes drifted shut, and she forced them open again. Jade grinned up at her and chattered something. She smiled and nodded, then held her head. Movement was not good.

A sound from the device told her Brennan had messaged.

"How is Jade doing?"

"Good. Still not much of an appetite," she voice-texted back.

"You?"

"I'm half-dead, but I'll be okay." She added a halfhearted smiling face, then set her book and the device aside.

Half an hour of feverish sleep later, she was aware of Jade climbing up to join her and felt more relaxed knowing where the toddler was. A few sounds came from the device, but she ignored them and fell back asleep.

Cold. Why was she cold? She sat up, frantic. "Where's Jade?" Kiera blinked quickly to clear her vision and saw the little girl helping Brennan put away dishes. He was home? What time was it?

Kiera pulled herself to her feet and shuffled to the kitchen. She caught the island counter and swayed from dizziness. Brennan dropped his dish towel and reached to steady her.

"Hey, what are you doing up?" His voice was gentle.

"Did you guys eat yet? I think there are leftovers." She pushed past him to the refrigerator.

"Kiera, we are fine." He fixed his eyes on her face, forcing her to look at him. "I'm just about to put Jade to bed. Promise me you'll stay on the couch, and I just might give you some dinner too." A little smile.

"Okay." She leaned her burning forehead against the cold metal refrigerator door. "I don't feel very good."

He led her to the couch, then disappeared upstairs to tuck Jade in. She was shivering when he returned, and he brought her a blanket and a bowl of soup.

Kiera tucked the blanket around herself and took a bite of soup. "Who made this? I didn't make it. This is really good. Why is this so good?" Another bite.

Brennan grinned. "I like cooking, and I thought maybe soup would help us get better faster."

"Well, you should have kept it a secret. I'm tempted to fake sickness sometime just to get more of that."

He took the empty bowl from her outstretched hands and carried it to the kitchen. Kiera laid back against the cushions, then shifted uncomfortably at the ache in her neck.

"So, now what do you want to do? I take it your headache won't let you read, and I'm not feeling so well, either." He sank down on the couch next to her and yawned.

She shrugged listlessly. "Do you want to watch a

movie? I have a few good ones on my device."

He answered by turning it on and scrolling through her movie collection. "How about this one? It looks fun."

Kiera nodded and sank back into the couch, struggling to keep her eyes open. She sagged against Brennan's shoulder, the weave of his T-shirt rough against her cheek. Looking up at him through the tangled curtain of hair, she smiled slightly when he looked at her.

Brennan reached to smooth her hair from her face but stopped short and turned back to the movie, shifting to make her more comfortable. Kiera's head was aching unbearably, but the steady hum of conversation in the movie lulled her to sleep.

She stirred when Brennan laughed at something. Blinking, she brushed the hair out of her eyes but didn't try to sit up. "Did I fall asleep?"

"Yes, but I can back it up if you want."

"No, it's okay." She sat up and focused on the movie. "I've seen it before."

"I can see why that was on your list of favorites. I've seen a lot by that director, but I can't believe I've missed this one," Brennan remarked when the movie was over.

Kiera half grinned. "Jordan and I can recite it to each other."

He smiled and shut the device. "Have you seen *October's Ride*? It's one of my favorites."

"No, wanna show it to me?"

"How does next Friday work for you?"

"I'll be here."

He reached a hand out to help her up, and she swayed slightly as dizziness set in once again. Wrapping the blanket tightly around herself, Kiera started up the stairs with him following closely to make sure she didn't fall.

Kiera rinsed the spaghetti sauce off her fingers and dried them on her apron. Pausing to check the device, she grinned when she noticed a message from Destiny.

Hi, you! Whatcha doing?"

She hurried to respond.

Just getting some cooking done while Brennan is at work and Jade is napping.

Destiny: Look at you, busy P31 woman!

Winking smiley faces.

Kiera: I've been wanting to get some cooking ahead in for a while but was too busy with sewing Easter dresses. And then we got the flu. I'm hoping this way I can send Brennan with meals, so he doesn't have to buy junk.

Destiny: Loved your dresses, by the way!

An elaborate string of heart-eyed smileys.

Hey, don't you have a nickname for him yet?

Kiera shook her head as she brought the cutting board over to the table so she could work and talk.

It's not nearly that cute over here.

That sounded snappish. Fortunately, messages didn't pick up on tone.

Destiny: Sorry.

Kiera: It's okay.

Good time to change the subject.

I was just remembering how fun our cosmetic making party was, and thought we should do something like that again soon.

Destiny: OOOOO!!! I'm in. Ideas??

Kiera: Definitely a mud fight.

Destiny: Okay. I think we have a few extra buckets in the barn.

Kiera: I was messing with you!

Laughing faces.

Count on old Des to make my prank backfire!

Kiera laughed and shook her head.

Kiera: I need to decorate my room and you're a wizard at that. Sooo… When should we do this? The evenings are always busy. Brennan likes the house quiet after a long day of work.

Destiny: What do you do?

Kiera: Um, we read like old friends.

Destiny: Sounds boring.

A tongue-sticking out smiley face followed quickly.

Kiera: Not when the 'ship' wars happen. He always has canon on his side though. He's read the series before, so he knows all the fan theories.

A hodgepodge of crying and laughing faces skipped onto the screen. Destiny's message followed.

I'm dying over here picturing it!!! I've always thought he was so serious.

Kiera laughed to herself. Scraping the chopped veggies into the soup pot, she added to the message stream.

Do you want to come some morning with your
fantastically weird scrap bag?

Destiny: Yes please. If you please, ma'am. I'll try
to be good.

Kiera: Hang on, dear. I'm getting a voice call.

The call dropped seconds later.

Never mind. I missed it, but Mom'll call back if
she needs.

Destiny: I was reading this really weird book the
other day...

Kiera: Aaaand Jade might be waking up, so
keep talking while I'm gone.

Kiera set a few large knives up on the high
counter, washed her hands again, and flew up the stairs
to the sound of several incoming messages. Wow,
Destiny was talking a lot. Her book must have been
really weird.

She listened at the nursery door and decided she
had just imagined Jade was awake. Back downstairs,
she poured the spaghetti sauce into jars to cool and
stirred the simmering soup. Now, what was a good
breakfast to make ahead?

The device chirped again, reminding her that

Destiny was still waiting. She looked at the most recent message.

> I am so sorry, dear. That must be so scary! I'm praying for you.

Kiera's heart jumped and fingers flew.

> Wait, what's going on? Is this a payback prank?

> Destiny: I don't think I should be the one to tell you. Maybe you should call your Mom back. Love you, dear.

No expression faces. Destiny was never this calm.

Kiera raced to check the voice calls. There were no messages left behind, but three missed calls were left in addition to Mom's first try. One was from Ian? He never called her. All of this had happened while she was upstairs? Her hands were shaking as she pushed the button to voice call Mom. No answer. She tried again. She even tried Dad and Ian. No one picked up. Should she call Jordan?

Brennan. "Pick up, oh, please pick up. If I don't find out what is going on…" She yelled at the device.

Brennan's voice cut through the speaker. "Kiera, I'm coming home right now."

"Brennan, what in the world is going on? Will you please tell me? I can't get ahold of anyone!"

"Your mom didn't tell you?!"

"I missed her calls!" she shrieked.

"You know Thorne was officiating that wedding today?" He was eerily calm. Just like Destiny. She could picture his face, completely at rest but pain in his eyes.

"Yes?" Kiera squeezed her thumb.

"It turned out to be a perverted relationship. He refused to officiate right there at the altar." He paused.

She sat down. Sucked in a breath. She knew what came next.

"The police picked him up on his way home. They have him at the station while they decide what to do with him."

"But he was so careful. He met them both beforehand and did their counseling. I don't understand. Is this a joke?"

"Shelby was just a hired actor. It was a setup to kick Thorne out."

She was sobbing now.

"Kiera, I'm coming home."

"I can't believe it." She stood up from the chair and went upstairs without ending the call.

Shutting both her bedroom door and the closet door against the unwelcome news, she burrowed back into her closet. The hems of her dresses brushed the top of her head as she drew in her knees and forced herself to breathe through the flood of tears. Heartbeats passed before she could think straight to pray.

"Lord God, why is this happening? You know

what this does to a pastor and his church. We were already hanging on by a thread, and now what? I know it's 'just jail', but I'm so afraid. And angry. Really angry. They did this on purpose, didn't they? To split the church because they don't agree with him. I'm sorry, but I can't seem to stop being angry. Will You help me stop somehow?"

She laid her head on her knees and started crying again. "I just want everything to be okay. I was so afraid of the draft, but You fixed that. You've given me Jade and Brennan's friendship, but what now?" She sucked in a sobbing breath. "Lord, please help me to be patient and still before You. Please help me to reach out to others and be a minister of peace."

Kiera breathed deeply and listened to the silence. A favorite song about sparrows being looked after by God came into her mind, and she rocked back and forth with the tune in her head.

"Kiera? Kiera, where are you?" Brennan's frantic voice came from the loft.

"I'm in here."

"Are you okay? I got here as fast as I could."

The panic and sorrow in his voice made her realize just what she had done to him. His best friend was going to jail, and she had only added to his concerns. "I'm so sorry," she whispered and stood up, twisting her ring.

Opening both sets of doors, she stood in the doorway and looked him full in the face as she wiped the tears away.

"I'm sorry you had to find out this way." He looked away and ran his fingers through his hair.

"No, I'm glad you told me." Time to help him. "I'm sorry I hid. It's something I do whenever I'm sad or afraid, but it wasn't fair to you. You didn't need me to add to your worry."

"You're okay. It's all okay." He reached out to her slightly, then let his arms drop and looked away. "They're all gathering at your parents' for prayer. Do you want me to take you?"

"Sure. Thank you."

"Okay." He took off his coat and laid it around her shoulders. "Get in the car, and I'll grab Jade."

CHAPTER FIFTEEN
Prayer

She zipped up his coat and shrank deeper into it as she waited in the car. The enormity of what had just happened still lingered in her mind, leaving her in a distracted haze, but she managed to speak when he started the engine.

"You doing okay?"

"It's really unexpected." He shook his head. "I'm just praying the judges are lenient and this doesn't affect the church too much."

Kiera nodded in reply. His factual breakdown of the situation and overall attitude was calming, and she laid a hand on his arm to steady them both for the rest of the drive.

"Are you coming inside?" Kiera hesitated as she got out of the car.

"No, I think it will be good for this to be a family thing," he replied, getting out to come over and talk to her. He shoved his hands deep into his pockets. It was unusually cold for this late in spring.

She nodded through the curtain of staticky hair that had fallen in her face.

"Stay as long as you like and call me when you want to come home."

She nodded again and managed to give him a small smile.

He laid a hand on her shoulder, and the surprise made her look up at him. "I'll be praying for you, Kiera."

She twisted her ring and whispered, "Thank you."

Kiera was shaking as she reached out to press the doorbell, but Brennan's car still sitting in the driveway filled her with courage, and she fought back the tears. She had asked God to help her be a minister of peace.

Jordan, looking gray with tiredness and twenty-six years of life, answered the door with his sleeping daughter in one arm. He pulled his little sister into a hug with his free arm.

She let herself cry into his shoulder for a moment before asking, "Where's Mom?"

"They're all in the living room. C'mon." He guided her to the couches with his arm around her shoulders, and she sat down near Mom, letting her grip her hand without speaking a word.

Dad was praying aloud. Kiera could never remember a word he said afterward, but she knew that God did, and this gave her peace. Ian prayed next and brought them all to tears, but she could only remember Rachel's hand on her shoulder as the family drew together in a tight group. Then suddenly she realized it was her turn to pray.

"Lord, I've been asking You all day for peace. Sometimes I think peace means having everything right in the world. Other times I think that peace is having everything right in our hearts. Whichever You give us, I know You will give one of them. And Lord, one of the biggest things I think we are all worried about is church. Lord, please help this not to turn anyone away from You. Please help us to grow stronger in faith and not to be bitter. In Jesus' name."

Church people dropped by throughout the night, but she barely noticed anyone except a tearful Jessica who only stayed for a few moments. She sat down on the floor in front of the couch and hugged her knees to herself. They were all here! Why couldn't Thorne be with them, and what was happening to him at the moment?

Madelyn ran by chasing her older brother, and the tears rose in Kiera's eyes at the memories it brought to mind. Thorne had always been there for her whenever she needed him, but now he was the one in trouble. All she could do was pray.

"Lord, I feel so helpless. There is really nothing I can do. I leave this in Your capable hands," she opened her fists, "and ask You to help me deal with the outcome. In Jesus' name."

Peace filled her, and she found the courage to

smile. One way or another, all would be well. Using the edge of the couch as a support, she stood up and slowly made her way upstairs, leaving the huddled group behind. She tiptoed through the loft, stepping over nieces and nephews in their rows of sleeping bags.

Quietly opening the door of her old room, Kiera turned on the light. The bed was still there, but a new lamp rested on the side table next to it. She sank into the pillow and pulled the covers up over herself in a half-asleep movement.

Kiera yawned and stretched. Her shadow stretched too, projected onto the wall by the morning sunshine. Shivering slightly in the cold room, she grabbed Brennan's jacket off the end of her bed and put it on. Pawing the wild mess that was her hair into a loose braid, she entered the loft. Only a few children still slept in the long row, and one of them stirred sleepily and opened his eyes to smile.

"Hey, Baron," she said, recognizing Ian and Rachel's youngest son. "Are you ready to get up?"

He reached out to put his arms around her neck, and she lifted him up. Soon enough his older brother and sisters would be awake, but for now he was her buddy. It was quiet downstairs, but Ian and Rachel moved around the kitchen talking in low tones.

"Good morning, Kiera," Rachel said, pulling her

into a hug when she noticed her.

"Good morning. Are Jordan and Niyanna still here?"

"They left a few hours ago so he could get home in time for work," Ian explained, taking the heavy toddler from her.

"Makes sense. Dad and Mom?"

"They're still sleeping. I think your prayer really helped them, Kiera, especially Mom. She was much more peaceful afterward and went to bed just a few hours later, although I don't think they'll be getting up anytime soon," Rachel said.

"We've decided to spend the day here to support them and let the kids rest a little more, though I see Mr. Early Bird here was excited for the morning." Ian tickled Baron, who giggled as Rachel joined in the game.

Kiera smiled at the sweet display of family affection. Loneliness washed over her like a flood. She missed Jade. She needed Brennan.

"I should be getting home soon, if you think that's okay. When Mom gets up, will you tell her I love her and to call me anytime?"

They answered by pulling her into a hug along with Baron, and the tears she had conquered the night before returned.

"It's okay, dear, and we'll deliver your message," Rachel said.

She pulled away and wiped her eyes with the

napkin Ian handed her. "Okay, I'll call Brennan."

Kiera sat on the floor with her legs stretched out in front of her and set the device on her lap. Being home was second nature to her, and she slipped back easily into old habits. She sent the request for a call and smoothed her loose braid.

"Hey, Brennan."

"How are you doing?" His voice was tired.

"I'm okay. Prayer last night really helped me find peace in the Lord, but it's like every little thing reminds me of what's happened. It's gonna be a hard couple of weeks coming up."

"Mmm. Yeah, we'll have to continue praying, won't we?" She knew without a doubt that the pause that came after was him running his fingers through his hair. "You ready to come home?"

"Yeah. I hope this doesn't make you late for work."

"No, it's okay. I took the day off anyway, since I can barely focus. See you in a few."

She stood up and tucked the device into her purse. Nieces and nephews clamored for breakfast and shouted good morning. Taking Baron back from Ian, she left mother and father to quiet their children and find food for all of them.

"Do you want some, Kiera?" Ian offered her dry cereal and a banana.

"No, I'm okay. I think that's Brennan in the driveway anyway." She stood up to look out the blinds.

Sliding Baron into the highchair, she said quick goodbyes and went outside to the sound of two children asking for seconds. Brennan was waiting for her at the car with a friendly smile, but she reached for the back door first and leaned in to hug Jade good morning.

"Hi, baby. Mommy missed you."

"I hash manna," Jade replied, holding up a rather mushed banana to show her.

"Nice. Is it yummy?"

Jade nodded and swung her legs happily. Kiera turned away with a smile and shut the door.

"I just had to say good morning to her. All the little kids at Dad and Mom's made me miss her quite a bit," she explained to Brennan as she got in the car.

"I gotcha." He ran a hand over his unshaven chin and programmed the car to drive home.

Kiera doubted he had slept at all the night before. "You know, you should have come in. People from church dropped by, and I'm sure no one would have minded you being there."

He shook his head and gave a little smile. "It's okay. Have you heard anything from Jessica?"

Her heart stopped and she turned to him. "Jessica? I think she was there but only for a moment. Why?"

"It's just she and Thorne...you know. I mean it's not like he's dead, but it's still got to be hard on her."

Kiera burst into tears and covered her face with

her hands. "I thought maybe, but I wasn't sure. I should have spoken to her."

"No, look, it's okay. I'm sorry I mentioned it."

"No, you're fine." She wiped her eyes with the coat sleeves that hung over her hands. "I'm acting like a child." She forced a smile and looked directly at him. "Tell me something happy."

"Um...I finished book four. Do you want to borrow it when we get home?"

"Yeah. I do." She yawned. "I should probably give your coat back someday, shouldn't I?"

CHAPTER SIXTEEN
A Faithful Few

It took Kiera over a week to finally message Jessica. A voice call would be too hard. For both of them.

> Hi Jessica! Since church is canceled, I thought I'd message you to say hey and catch up a little. I'm sorry I barely noticed you at the prayer meeting—I was only thinking of myself, which is pretty selfish of me.

She picked up a skirt she was mending and leaned back in her chair to wait for Jessica's reply.

> Kiera! No worries. I'm sure this is a very hard time for your family, and I want you to know that Papa and I are praying for you. I was very shaken up those first few days; but God has everything in control, and He gives sweet people like you to message me.

> Kiera: Aw, you're sweet.

Jessica: So, what keeps you busy?

Kiera had never talked to Jessica much before. She had only been back at church for a year and, being a lot older, tended to hang out with the women of the church. Only recently had Kiera officially become part of that group. This conversation was turning out a lot better than she had expected. She typed back.

Oh, Jade mostly (she's my two-year-old), as well as regular housework. I really enjoy gardening, and I treat myself to some reading in the evenings. And I also keep a public journal like once in a blue moon. How about you?

Jessica: Wow, a two-year-old sounds fun! I have housework like you do and Papa to keep company, but the rest of my time is spent with the pro-life ministry. I'm not doing much right now, since Thorne is unable to guide me; but when things settle down a little bit, we'll visit him and talk about next steps. Right now I'm focusing on raising awareness of embryo adoption.

Kiera: Sounds like a nice mix! What specifically are you raising awareness of and how can I help you?

Jessica: The pool of embryos to adopt from is steadily growing, especially as more mothers are drafted and don't come home. You don't mind me talking about this, do you? It's just part of my life.

Kiera swallowed and sent the message.

No, you're fine.

Jessica: Anyway, they range in age from conception to about a week old. People don't usually think of adopting them because it's more trouble and quite little known, but the need is real. The health facilities are only 'able' to store them for two years, and who knows when that time frame will decrease.

Kiera read her next words through tears.

Jessica: If we can't save other babies, we can at least save these.

Kiera: I am so glad you are doing this, Jessica! I never knew this much about your ministry, and I think it's beautiful the way you are working to save the least of these. What can I do to help? Write a journal post? Bang on doors?

Jessica replied with a smiling face.

Thank you for your encouragement. A journal post would be great, but I think banging on doors would be a little too out there. If you think adoption is something your family would like to do, talk to your husband about it, and I'll connect you with the right people. Here's the link to the health facility site for starters.

She jerked upright and stared across the room at Brennan's profile for a moment. He was deep in Bible study homework. Kiera herself was already an unusual addition to his life, but a baby? How could she even ask for one?

She forced herself not to accidentally type what she was thinking.

Thanks, Jessica. Have you heard anything about church?

Jessica: Services have been canceled while they look for an interim pastor, but Papa and I are inviting anyone who wants to come over for worship at our house.

"Brennan, come look at this," Kiera called across the room, hiding the message about adoption with a few swift clicks. That would just be too awkward if he saw it.

"What is it?" He came over to stand behind her and scanned Jessica's message about church. "Ask her what time."

Jessica's reply bounced in in moments.

Just a warning that we're pretty slim on members right now, but a few families have agreed to meet at our house this Thursday at six-ish if you want to come.

She looked up at Brennan. He nodded. "We'll be there."

Kiera: We'd love to come. Thanks for inviting us, Jessica.

Jessica: You're welcome. Have a great evening!

Kiera: You too.

Kiera turned around in her chair to look at Brennan. "Proud of me for messaging her?" she asked playfully.

He grinned and shook his head. "You should have voice called her."

"We would have both been crying if I had done that."

He shrugged. "Come read with me?"

"No spoilers on the next book?"

"Solemn promise."

Kiera hurried into her church clothes and tied her headcovering on over half-combed hair. It felt odd going to church on a Thursday evening, but the biggest issue was being ready right after Brennan arrived home from work. Running down the stairs, she met him coming up to do the minimum of shaving and changing his shirt.

"That food smells done."

"I hear ya."

She reached the kitchen just in time to open the oven and pull out the pan of squash before it browned any further. Covering the pan with a lid to hold in the heat, she placed it in an insulated bag on the counter and checked that the crock of rice was staying warm.

Jade wandered over from playing with her dolls as Kiera began slicing a loaf of almond bread.

"I has bread, pleash?"

"You can have some later when we get to church."

Jade's face crunched up, and she grunted angrily.

"Jade, be sweet."

"No," Jade said, looking at her to see what she would do.

Okay, they could be late to church. "Jade," she warned.

"No, I has bread now." It was a rare treat.

Kiera calmly gathered the bread up into a bag and set it on the counter with the rest of the food, then took Jade's hand in hers and led her upstairs to the nursery where she administered correction.

"Jade, Mommy says to wait for bread. Say 'yes, Mommy'."

The toddler swallowed her defiance with a lot of tears. "Yes, Mommy."

"Good girl!" Kiera beamed and gave her a hug. "Now, let's get your hair all pretty for church and join Daddy."

They were only a few minutes late to church as they joined four other cars in front of Pastor Silas's house.

"We've never done church this way; this ought to be interesting," Brennan said as he unbuckled Jade, set her down on the sidewalk near him, and then reached back for the crock. "It's good, though."

"I hope so. There aren't very many people here, are there? Do you see the Moores?" Kiera replied, holding the squash in one hand and the bread in the other. "Hold on to Mommy's skirt, Jade."

"No, I don't, but here come your parents," he announced as another car pulled up and parked along the street.

They waited outside to let the Clarks catch up so they could all enter together. Kiera studied her parents as they waited on the porch. Dad's hair was grayer in a few places, and Mom looked as if she hadn't slept well in a while; but they gave her brave smiles whenever their eyes met. She looked at Brennan winding up the crock cord so it wouldn't drag and Jade holding obediently on to her skirt. So much had changed in such a short time.

Jessica opened the door with a very smiley welcome. "Hello, all! Here, Mr. Clark, let me take that from you," she said, reaching for the foil pan he carried and leading the way to the kitchen.

"Sorry we're late," Kiera apologized, setting down the bags she carried.

"Oh, no, that's okay. We haven't even started yet. You can put the bread out here on the table," Jessica offered, scooting two plates of dessert aside to make room.

"Any news on who the church chose as an interim pastor?" she asked as she took off her coat and caught Jade.

Jessica hand-combed her bangs aside and looked troubled. "They chose one with a doctorate who is highly approved by the denomination, but wouldn't be by us. She performed the ceremony a week after Thorne refused to."

Kiera shook her head and hot tears came into her eyes. She fought hard to force bitterness aside.

"Fortunately, not everyone is on board with the idea, but Papa will explain that more later," Jessica added.

"That's good," was all Kiera could think to say. Her eyes wandered to the living room where people shuffled around to find places to sit. "I should join Brennan."

She slid into the folding chair next to him and gripped the edges to keep herself from shaking.

"Kiera, what's wrong?" Brennan asked in an undertone.

She avoided looking at him and inclined her head toward Pastor Silas instead. "He'll say in a minute."

Pastor Silas rose from his chair and stood in the middle of the room to address them. The burden from many years of ministry caused him to stoop forward, but his eyes still shone with passion and zeal for the Lord's work. His feathery white hair stood out slightly above his ears, and he wore his Sunday best exactly the way she had always remembered him.

"I'm not feeling well enough this evening to give you a proper sermon, but I thought we would treat it like family devotions and share a time of prayer and study. But before we get started, I wanted to let you know what is going on with the church." He sighed and put his fingertips together. "In a meeting last evening, a majority of the church board chose an interim pastor. She holds a doctorate from one of the denomination's finest schools, but she also performed the very act Pastor Thorne refused to do."

Murmurs went through the crowd of six families gathered in the small living room. Kiera swallowed down the sick feeling that had risen within her, and Brennan wrinkled his brow as he took in this new information.

"These actions are in direct opposition to what I

believe from Scripture and what our pastor is now serving jail time to stand up for. I couldn't in good conscience continue on the board, and I handed in my letter of resignation soon after the announcement, as did Deacon White," he nodded toward the middle-aged man and his family, then to a young man sitting nearby, "and Deacon Tiegler."

The families were quiet, and looking at their faces Kiera knew the concern in their eyes was over the state of their church and not in disagreement. She turned to look at Brennan to see his reaction, but he only nodded at her.

"Looks like we'll be meeting in houses like this for a while. I just hope more families have the faith to join us," Brennan whispered.

She swallowed and stroked Jade's curls. Would Thorne find any church when he returned?

"Let's pray," Deacon White said, breaking the heavy silence.

Pastor Silas sighed as he took a chair, and the light seemed to go out of his eyes for a moment. Kiera nodded and said amen over and over in her heart as the prayers of the saints rose up to their Father, asking for the purity of the church and His sustaining hand to be with their leaders.

"Lord, I pray for my wife Kiera…"

Her eyes flew open and she stared at Brennan for a moment, then forced herself to clamp them shut again.

"Lord, help her to be strong in You, and Lord,

give her peace. Thank you for the way You have already enabled her to strengthen others in You, Lord."

His words reached out to her, filling her with hope and warmth, and she held them tight to her as the evening went on.

CHAPTER SEVENTEEN
Flicker

"It looks like the Apple Valley and Munroe farms are having the blight, but Tatler has everything but eggs. Well, they have them; but Mom told me they are free-range, and not very much care is taken to make sure they aren't contaminated by radiation." Kiera leaned on her elbows and stared at the agricultural map on her device. The longer the war stretched on, the more contaminated the food supply got.

Brennan turned away from fixing himself a cup of coffee. "Any farms nearby where we could pick up eggs?"

"The Moores' is the only one I can think of," she answered.

"Why don't we stop by there?"

"Sounds perfect, and maybe we'll get to do a little catching up with them." She smiled in anticipation.

His smile told her she had hit upon exactly what he was thinking. He had been looking for a way to get her and Destiny together since they didn't see each other at church anymore.

"I'll need to make a shopping list and get Jade ready, but I think I can be ready to go anytime after that."

"Does half an hour sound good?"

"Deal."

She inventoried the pantry and the fridge, then went upstairs to wake Jade.

"Hey, girly," she said as she scooped her out of the crib.

In a flash, she had replaced pajamas with a dress, leggings, and practical rain boots, then twisted her hair into pigtails and buttoned a snuggly sweater.

"Now for Mommy," she said, setting Jade on her bed so she could change clothes in the closet.

Her favorite plaid shirt beckoned to her, and she grinned as she paired it with boots and a paneled denim skirt. She felt like dressing as a farmgirl today. Ten minutes left on the half hour. She could spare a few minutes to braid her hair in double french braids.

Talking to Jade all the while, Kiera carefully pulled her hair into two braids, then frowned at herself in the mirror. Already the nine-year age gap between her and Brennan was slightly dramatic, but this hairstyle made her look even younger than her actual age. She twisted the braids around her head and held them in place with a few hairpins. Applying a little makeup for good measure, she took Jade downstairs to wait for

Brennan.

Mother and daughter were sitting on the couch together browsing through a picture book when he found them.

Kiera looked up to see his eyes on them and gave a teasing smile. "Coming with us, city boy?"

He grinned at her and pointed toward his sports shoes. "These don't count?"

"Okay, maybe." She took Jade's hand and followed him out the door, excitement for the day building within her.

It died slightly when Brennan parked the truck outside Tatler Farms and turned to her awkwardly. "This is a Muslim neighborhood, so a hijab might be a good idea." He shrugged. "Or if you wanted to stay in the car with Jade…"

Kiera squeezed her thumb. "No, it's okay. I'll wear one; I've done it before. I'd rather come with you."

She opened her purse and pulled out a black scarf, then looked up instructions to help her remember. It was pretty similar to tying her own headcovering, but the meaning it carried was nothing alike. She hated playing the part, but it was safer. Good thing she had already put her hair up today; it made everything go much more smoothly.

"Does it look right to you?" She turned to Brennan, who was patiently waiting.

He nodded. "Do you have a long-sleeved sweater or something you could wear?"

She pulled it on and grabbed her purse.

Brennan carried Jade, but Kiera walked close to him, avoiding the gazes of the men who stared at her openly. On the way back to the truck, she hid behind Jade's head and a small crate of fruit as she followed Brennan. Sliding his boxes into the back seat with Jade, he took the crate from her and offered an encouraging smile.

The second Kiera was in the cab of the truck, she jerked the hijab off with a sigh of relief and stuffed it into her purse. Neither she nor Brennan spoke for the rest of the car ride. Jade just sucked her thumb.

They pulled into the Moores' driveway, and the truck hummed to a polite stop. Destiny shrieked and ran toward it, dropping her pitchfork as she went. The resident farm dog announced their arrival to anyone who would listen. Kiera opened the side door and stepped down into the dusty driveway seconds before her friend pulled her into a crushing hug.

"Oh my goodness, dear! You nearly gave me a heart attack when I recognized the truck. What are you all doing out this way?" She brushed a dark strand of hair out of her eyes. Her shirt was all ruffles and sparkles, but her cuffed jeans were faded and grass-stained.

"The farms we usually go to are having the blight, so we went to Tatler today instead; but they didn't have good eggs, so here we are," Kiera explained with a wide smile.

"And anyway, we like giving out heart attacks to people who run with pitchforks," Brennan said from next to Kiera.

Both girls pretended to frown at him.

"Daddy, yook! Is that a cow?" Jade pointed.

"Go buy eggs from my brother, Brennan, while I borrow these lovely ladies," Destiny ordered.

He shrugged helplessly and handed Jade over to Kiera, then set off for the porch. The "ladies" turned toward the barn, and Kiera was suddenly very glad of her boots when it got sloppier from the animal muck. She giggled to herself over Brennan's choice of shoes and noticed her friend trying her best to ignore it.

Halfway to the barn, Destiny broke. "How is it going with you and Brennan?"

Kiera shrugged. "Fine. We're friends."

Destiny looked at her reproachfully. "That'll never do. I haven't seen you in weeks, remember?"

"He's been really kind to me about Thorne, and I think we understand each other slightly better because of it. That's really all though." She played with one of her buttons. "I've missed seeing you."

Destiny studied the tire ruts for a moment, then decided to answer the unspoken question. "Dad says he's done." She looked up at Kiera. Tears glittered in her dark-brown eyes. "We don't really see him much anymore except for a few nights of the week. Mom isn't against God, but she's been 'getting her church in' by listening to motivational speakers. She says it's a lot safer that way, and she can get a new pastor whenever she wants one with just a few clicks. And Kent, well, I'm not sure what he thinks. Aric and I want to come to church, but we haven't been allowed to."

"Destiny, I'm so sorry! I'll definitely be praying for you all," Kiera said earnestly, setting Jade down to put an arm around her friend.

"Thank you." Destiny wiped her eyes. "Come on, I really brought you in here to see the kittens."

Just then, one blurred by in a ball of fur, and Jade took off chasing it.

"Kiera, catch Myles!" Destiny directed, pointing to the chubby gray kitten escaping into the hay and taking off after another one.

Kiera caught the kitten by his back legs and swooped him up into her arms. He melted and began to purr, his blue eyes large and soft. Destiny came up with a kitten in each arm, and Jade followed juggling another.

"Yook, Mommy! I has kitten."

"Yes! Good job. Be careful with him." She reached out to steady the kitten.

Destiny caught her breath. "Seriously, dear, you should loan me your girly more often. She is a workout and a comedy show at the same time."

"Naw, I'd miss her too much." Kiera tousled Jade's curls fondly. "So, introduce the kittens to me."

"You are holding Myles, Sir Myles actually. He's the cuddliest of them all. I have," she glanced down at the balls of fur in her arms, "Widget and Elissa, or 'Lisers' if you are Aric. And Jade has Flicker, who is Widget's practical twin."

"I love them all," Kiera said.

"Take them all," Destiny offered, pretending to push two more kittens at her.

"I don't think Brennan would go for that," she laughed.

"I'll convince him." Destiny was already outside before she could say another word.

"C'mon, Jade. It's probably time to go anyway." Kiera laid a hand on her daughter's shoulder and guided her out of the barn.

"The kitty ish sleeping," Jade said, looking up at her.

She laid a kiss on the toddler's head and half-hoped Destiny's mission would work. Halfway across the field, she shaded her eyes and grinned at the farmhouse front porch. Brennan was running his fingers through his hair and shaking his head, and Aric was laughing as Destiny gave an emphatic speech.

"Help me out here, Kiera," Brennan said as she joined him on the porch.

"We don't need four kittens, Destiny. We have a two-and-a-half-year-old," she said.

"Who happens to be sweetly holding a sleeping kitten at this moment." Destiny arched her eyebrows.

Kiera looked up at Brennan. "She has a point."

He groaned.

"Daddy, yook! The kitty is fuwwy!" Jade shoved Flicker at him.

"Yeah, Princess." He grinned down at her, then straightened. "Destiny Moore, Kiera Stewart, it's been nice knowing you, and for the record you did not convince me; but I think it would be good for Jade to grow up with a pet, and she seems pretty smitten with this one."

"Softie," Aric teased and punched him in the shoulder.

"One kitten named Flicker and three dozen eggs sold to Brennan Stewart," Destiny intoned.

"I guess this is our cue to leave then," Brennan replied, handing the kitten back to Jade and taking the eggs from Aric.

Kiera set down the yawning Myles, who scampered after his remaining siblings, and hugged Destiny goodbye. "So good to see you, friend."

"You too, dear."

"You're still coming to help me decorate my room, right?"

"You betcha."

"Jade, say 'thank you' to the Moores for the kitty," Kiera prompted.

"Thank you," Jade said.

"Aw, you come visit your aunt Destiny again soon! Okay, dear?" Destiny melted, giving the toddler a squeeze.

Everyone laughed, and Brennan shook hands with Aric before stepping down from the porch to walk over to the truck. Kiera and Jade followed with Destiny giving a parting shot of a whispered, "You two are so cute together."

Kiera just grinned and shook her head.

Turning to Brennan in the car, she said, "Thanks for the trip, softie. I think it did Destiny and me both good."

"You're welcome. I'm glad I made it out alive with just one kitten. And by the way, that's the second time you've called me a name today."

She grinned at the windshield and twisted her ring. They were officially cute together.

Kiera yawned as the purring ball of fluff curled up on her shoulder. At least Flicker hadn't chosen to sleep in the middle of her book. When he wasn't busy playing with the toy Jade dragged for him or hiding when he was tired of her, the kitten was a cuddly addition to the family. The relaxing evening before her looked especially inviting after a full day of homemaking. Cleaning the rest of the house could wait.

She looked up at Brennan, who had abandoned his book and was glancing absently around the room as he drank a glass of water. Draining it, he said, "It looks nice in here. Not much left to do before church tomorrow, eh?"

"No, but what does that have to do with church?" A sudden thought hit her. "Oh, no! You did not! Are we hosting church tomorrow?"

"Yes, I volunteered at our last meeting, and didn't I tell you?" Brennan raised his eyebrows quizzically.

"No, you didn't say a word about it. Some warning would have been really good." She felt like crying, but frustration swallowed her tears. Sitting up on her knees, she glared at him over the back of the couch. "Brennan, I'm the youngest married woman in church, practically still a child, and *I'm* hosting?"

"We're hosting."

She threw a couch pillow at him. And then another. Somewhere in between those was a jumble of insecure generalities about having the wrong tablecloth, the mop not working, and having to follow up "Mrs. White's stunning entertaining skills". Brennan caught the pillows and waited for her to calm down.

"I'm really sorry, Kiera. I should have remembered. But I'm here to help you with whatever you need. We can do some cleaning tonight, and I'll try to get off early from work tomorrow." He dropped the pillows. "All it really needs in here is a kitchen revamp and some vacuuming."

He was being maddeningly factual again, and she wasn't quite ready to let it go. Throwing a third couch pillow in his face, she stood up and started toward the kitchen, wordlessly tying an apron on over her clothes. She was halfway through fishing out vegetable scraps from the sink when she felt Brennan leaning on the counter next to her.

"I'm serious. What can I do?" he asked with a sincerity that made her feel ashamed.

"I'm sorry. I just didn't want to clean tonight, and all of those things I said were real insecurities, but it was no excuse to get angry at you." She squeezed her thumb underwater. "I'm really sorry."

"It's okay. Call it pax?" he asked, grinning at the reference to the books they were reading.

"Yeah." She smiled and gave him a soggy handshake.

Minutes later, the conversation faded to a memory to blush at in Kiera's mind. She was building a towering stack of dishes when a sigh of frustration caused her to turn around.

"Well, this mop is hopeless. I was using rubber bands for a while, but apparently no go. Guess I'll just have to ruin some washcloths. Can you toss me one?"

Kiera sent a washcloth flying across the room to him, and he caught it gratefully. Filling a bowl with hot soapy water, she set it down on the ground near him, then plunged her own washcloth into the water. They scrubbed along next to each other in companionable silence until the whole floor was sparkling.

"I hope that kitten isn't wrecking something somewhere," she yawned to Brennan as she rinsed their washcloths and squeezed them out.

"She's in here. Look." He motioned her over to the living room.

Jade had left a pile of dolls in one corner, and Flicker was burrowed in, sleeping deeply. Kiera grinned and yawned again. Stopping herself from leaning into him, she asked, "I guess that just leaves the vacuuming for tomorrow, right?"

Brennan nodded as he looked around the room.

"Thanks for helping me." She gave him a small smile.

"Anytime." He looked down at her and returned the gesture easily.

CHAPTER EIGHTEEN
Hosting Church

Kiera tucked a doll under each arm and scooped up the rest, juggling them as she ran upstairs to the sound of Brennan vacuuming. Opening Jade's door, she was relieved to find her still sitting in the middle of the floor, reading a picture book upside down.

"Hey, big girl! Are you ready to go downstairs for a snack before church?" She tweaked one of her curly pigtails.

Jade immediately dropped her book and reached up to be carried. Kiera hoisted the little girl onto her hip and went back downstairs. Brennan turned off the vacuum and rolled it into the front closet. The oven announced that its cooking time was finished.

"Brennan, would you mind taking that out?" Kiera asked as she peeled a banana and handed it to Jade.

He nodded, and she leaned against the table, stopping to take a breath and run through her mental task list. She turned to look at the oven and suddenly realized just how late it was now she could see the clock.

"The beans need to cook for ten more minutes… I'm ready except my headcovering… Mom and Dad are bringing extra chairs…" she mumbled aloud.

"Anything else I can help with?" Brennan asked from behind her. He ran his fingers through his wet hair, destroying the work of his comb.

"No, I'm sure I'm forgetting something, but I can't imagine what," she said, then added with a tired smile, "Thanks for coming home early."

"You're welcome. Now it's time for you to sit down and spend the next…" he checked his device, "six minutes before people arrive just being peaceful."

She smiled wryly at his word choice but knew he was right. Sitting down at the table, she smoothed back her hair and tied on her headcovering, willing herself to not be so nervous. He flopped down in a chair next to her.

"I don't exactly know everyone from church the way you do. Thorne's been my only friend for a while, so this ought to be interesting," Brennan said.

"I've always been a kid though, so we're about in the same boat." Kiera tucked a strand of hair behind her ear.

"Well, if you're feeling awkward or nervous, you're always welcome to join my conversations."

"Okay." She smiled. "Same to you."

Just a few minutes and several arrivals later, Kiera

discovered what she had been forgetting. Leaving Brennan to greet everyone and fit all the food on the table, she stood in the kitchen, patiently holding a pitcher for the filtered water to trickle into and shaking her head over her amateur hostess skills.

"Kiera!" Destiny surprised her with a hug from behind, and she nearly dropped the pitcher.

"Hi, Destiny! I'm so glad you could come," Kiera said, smiling widely at her friend and giving her a one-armed hug.

She noticed with surprise that Kent and Aric were standing in the kitchen as well and gave them a hearty hello.

"Where do you want this, Kier?" Aric asked, holding up a pan of lasagna.

"Oh, if you step into the dining room," she gestured over the kitchen bar, "Brennan will tell you where there's room. I'd help you, but I'm stuck in here for now since I forgot water."

"Where is Jade? I have to squeeze her," Destiny said, following her youngest brother out of the kitchen. "Kent, you gotta see her with the kitten."

Kent stayed leaning against the counter and watching the pitcher slowly fill as if it were the most interesting thing in the world. The kitchen clock filled the silence with its incessant ticking.

"So, how have you been?" Kiera found the courage to ask.

"All right, I guess." He shrugged carelessly but

something about him seemed on edge. "How's it going with you and old man Stewart?"

She grinned. "Kent, he's only twenty-seven."

"Oh, yeah, that's right. Just above draft age." He pulled on his ear where an earring had been removed for church.

"What are you bitter about? You're flat-footed—you'll never be drafted." Kiera made an effort at friendly teasing, but the angry look he had given her the first Sunday after she had married suddenly came to mind.

He shrugged. "You dodged it pretty well yourself."

They were back to talking about her and Brennan. Again. She studied him for a moment, and his expression made her heart sink. This was not the boy she had grown up with. A self-satisfied young man had replaced him.

"Kiera," he said softly.

She stiffened.

"If you ever get tired of this ludicrous half-marriage, I'd still—"

She set the pitcher down with a bang and turned on him with hot, angry tears spilling into her voice. She kept her volume low, knowing there were others nearby who could hear them. "I know what you are going to say, and I ask you to never say it again. Never say it, Kent Moore! Brennan and I are married for life, and not you or anyone should even suggest breaking that vow. You may not see it, but let me tell you there is respect and love even—yes, love!—in this relationship. Don't *ever* say it again!"

"Listen to you. Defending your decision with hypocritical happiness." Kent's words held an edge, and his eyes glinted dangerously.

Kiera looked him full in the face and was no longer angry. She shook from speaking so passionately, but she wasn't angry. She was only grieved and slightly afraid of what he would say next. She took the full pitcher and tried to move past him.

"Thorne gave up his career to skip officiating one wedding, but he did another one just as absurd." Kent crossed his arms and shook his head. "One word for why my church and my family are crumbling: hypocrites. My church pretended to love each other. My parents pretended to love each other too. Now look where everyone is today."

Kiera clenched her teeth and forced herself not to answer him. Tears threatened to stream down her face.

"Kiera, do you have the water yet?" Brennan met her in the doorway.

"Yes, here it is."

She held the pitcher out to him, but he paused and looked at her searchingly. Brennan's gaze swept past her to Kent leaning belligerently against the counter, then back to her face. His fingertips touched hers around the pitcher. "You okay?"

"Yeah, just a disagreement, that's all," she tried to reassure him.

"Your mom's here now, and she had a question for you. I forgot what it was."

"Thanks for telling me; I'll go catch up with her." She gave him a grateful smile and joined her church family in the living room.

Jade wiggled farther into the couch next to Kiera and leaned her head against Brennan. Putting her thumb into her mouth, she flopped over and shut her eyes. Afternoon church was late for her, and eating dinner beforehand made her even more sleepy. Kiera reached out to fondle her curls absently as she listened to Pastor Silas.

"'These things I have spoken to you, that in Me you may have peace. In the world you will have tribulation; but be of good cheer, I have overcome the world.' Now let's look at this in context. Jesus has just been telling them of the persecution to come; but mixed into it is the blessing that He knows, that He has provided a Helper for us, and that these momentary sorrows will be turned to everlasting joy. Let's thank Him for these blessings and pray for the days ahead."

Kiera bowed her head and folded her hands tightly together. What was there to fear? Christ had overcome the world. She knew that she feared Thorne being jailed for life, but the Helper reminded her He was with Thorne too. She feared what would happen to her friends if they continued to grow further away from God, but her prayers turned to asking the Lord to keep them.

With the last amen, she opened her eyes only to meet Kent's darkened gaze. Her last fear hit her with a ton of force. Was the tiny seed of love she had for Brennan enough to justify this marriage to him? Or was she just the hypocrite Kent was claiming her to be?

"Look at Jade," Brennan said with a smile in his voice. "She's out."

"I'll go tuck her in," Kiera offered, standing up and scooping the toddler into her arms.

Removing Jade's church shoes, she laid her down in the crib and spread a soft blanket over her. "Goodnight, girly," she said, kissing the mop of curls.

Sinking down with her back against the other crib, she turned her heart again to God and held this last fear out to Him.

"Dear Father, I asked You about this and You said yes. Please help me not to doubt my decision or blame myself for Kent's bitterness. Draw him back to You, please, Father. When I told him I loved Brennan, it was true. And it's becoming even truer every day, but please help me not to expect anything in return from Brennan and continue to love him in the way You choose. Thank you for Jade. Amen."

She stood up and dried a few stray tears on the back of her hand. Kiera closed Jade's door behind her and crossed the loft to her own room. Grabbing a cool cloth, she sat down at her desk and wiped the smudged makeup from her cheeks, then reapplied mascara and eyeliner. Readjusting her headcovering, she entered the warm, lively fellowship downstairs.

Kiera joined Pastor Silas at the table where he was choosing a dessert. "Pastor, I wanted to thank you for your sermon. It gave me a lot to think about. I've been giving in to fear lately, and I needed the reminder to bring it all to God."

"God be praised, Kiera," he said, placing a worn hand on her shoulder. "I've been praying so hard for this flock, but especially you and your family. It brings me great joy to hear that you are communing with our Lord. Thorne would be very pleased as well."

Kiera smiled slightly. "How is he?"

"He's doing all right. The stress tired him out a bit, but he's in good spirits," Pastor Silas answered.

"That's good to hear," Kiera said. She had only been allowed to face call her brother since his arrest—probably something to do with her age or relation—but the few leaders left in the church visited with him weekly.

He returned to his seat on the couch, listening to Kiera's mom and Jessica discussing growing squash. Kiera smiled to see them focusing on something other than Thorne's arrest. Her eyes searched the room for Brennan, and she found him trying to make conversation with Deacon and Mrs. White, who had hosted the last service. From the way he shifted from one foot to the other, she knew at once he was feeling shy. Swallowing down her own feelings, she made her way over to the group.

"Mind if I join you?" she asked Mrs. White quietly.

"Oh, not at all! My husband was just explaining the research he's been doing on self-driving car improvements for his job," Mrs. White filled her in on the conversation.

Of course it would be a topic she knew nothing about. She was no help to this conversation and would be just as useful in the backyard throwing a baseball with her dad and Aric. Farther away from Kent's sullen looks. She reached to grip her thumb, but Brennan gently forced her fingers open and laced his own through hers. The cold metal of his ring brought his words the night before to mind, and she let herself relax. *We're hosting.*

The conversation lagged for a moment, and she decided to interject. "You all did such a beautiful job hosting last week, we were slightly intimidated to follow you."

"Oh, not really? I'm glad you thought it was beautiful because the process of getting there was quite messy." Mrs. White giggled and looked at her husband.

"I smell a story," Kiera said, turning to Brennan.

He smiled at the Whites, and his hand slid out of hers and into his pocket.

"Yep, it's not every day your oven door falls off,"

Mr. White said dryly and scratched his beard.

"Or the service is down, so you have to call a friend to help put it back together. What a day!" Mrs. White added.

The conversation turned to their own personal infamous kitchen disasters, and Kiera found herself laughing and talking like an old friend with the woman she had been most intimidated to host. The conversation grew even more comfortable when Destiny joined with her own collection of mishaps and a few pranks. Mrs. White made them promise to come for tea sometime, and the conversation continued so delightfully Kiera barely noticed when Brennan and Mr. White slipped away to join the baseball game.

CHAPTER NINETEEN
Thorne

Kiera dumped a basketful of laundry onto the kitchen table and set the empty container in a nearby chair. Spying a pair of matching socks, she rolled them together and spiked them expertly into the basket. Pulling one of Jade's dresses out of the pile, she set it aside when she remembered how short it was getting. It was nearly time to sew again, and the coming palette was her favorite.

The device chirped the time and she glanced at it hopefully. It had taken a week of paperwork to approve a face call with Thorne, and she didn't want to miss a moment of the quarter hour the government had agreed to. The time was still a long way off, so she turned back to folding laundry and listening to the silent house.

"Mommy!"

She breathed a sigh of relief when she heard that Jade was awake and hurried up the stairs to get her buddy.

"I fold the laundry?" Jade asked when she saw the mound on the table.

"Yes, girly, you can help Mommy," Kiera said, untangling herself from Jade's dress and setting her down.

The toddler ran to the table and climbed onto a chair. Kiera handed her a washcloth and helped her fold it.

"Okay, now put it in the drawer," she directed.

They folded several dish towels together with Jade running them to the kitchen and standing on tiptoe to tuck them into their drawer. Each time she returned to the table, she gave Kiera a cheesy grin that made them both giggle.

Kiera was just stacking the laundry in the basket when the device sang out an incoming face call. She hurried to sit down and answer the call as Jade climbed into her lap and settled down. She held her breath for the split second it took for Thorne's face to appear on the screen.

Jade squealed and pointed, causing both brother and sister to laugh before falling silent to just look at each other. Thorne was exactly how Pastor Silas had described him—a little older, a little grayer, but in good spirits.

"How are you doing?" Kiera asked, twisting one of Jade's curls around her finger.

"All right. Not much has happened since you

called last week. It gets lonely, but I'm on good terms with a few others here; and I do get my visits and face calls." He winked in the old way.

"Any opportunities?"

"Not many. The first week they'd ask me what I was in for, and when I told them they'd shrug it off as a story. I think my lack of swear words is starting to convince them, though."

Kiera smiled at that.

"How are you doing?"

"Oh, we're doing fine. I've been keeping up on cooking ahead, which has been nice, and Jade helped me with laundry today. You should have seen how cute she was running dishcloths to the kitchen to put them away. Quite the go-getter. Brennan took us to the Moores' farm the other weekend, and we got a kitten for Jade."

"The kitty is fuwwy! I likes to play with him," Jade interrupted, bouncing up and down.

"Oh, really?" Thorne winked. "What color is the kitty?"

"Um…" She looked at her mommy.

"Flicker is gray," Kiera prompted.

"Yesh," Jade grinned. "The kitty is gway."

"Do you want to get her to show Uncle Thorne?" Kiera asked, and Jade slid off her lap to run and find the kitten.

She leaned her elbows on the table and thought through what was important enough to spend these precious moments telling her brother. "Oh, and I forgot to mention that we hosted one of the meetings. I was naturally nervous, but it ended up being a very encouraging time. Pastor Silas's sermon really helped me face some fears I've been struggling with lately." She wiped away a stray tear.

"I'm really glad to hear that, Kiera. Pastor Silas and Jessica have told me about some of the meetings, which is always encouraging. And before you razz me about Jessica—she comes to check in with me about the pro-life ministry. And yes, we are pursuing the Lord's will about deepening our relationship."

Kiera squealed and covered her mouth with both hands. "Oh, I have been waiting for this!"

Thorne's face broke into a smile, and he laughed out loud. "Now, before you name our children, it's just the early stages of courtship, and we haven't really told anyone yet."

"Oh, oh, oh! Is it okay if I tell Brennan about it, or do you want to wait until his call is approved and tell him yourself?"

Thorne grinned. "You can tell him. How is the old man, anyway?"

"Speak for yourself," Kiera teased, twisting her ring. "He's doing all right. I really hope he brings a new mop home. We were down on our hands and knees getting ready for church."

Her brother got a teasing look in his eyes. "Sounds like more to the story there, but I have to go now.

Love you, sis."

"Love you too, bro."

Jade ran up with the kitten to wave and yell, "Bye!"

The kitchen felt lonely after the call ended, but Kiera chose to hold on to the happy glow of Thorne's announcement. Stowing away the laundry, she next turned her hand to preparing dinner. Brennan would be home anytime now.

"I help?" Jade asked, and Kiera gave her a chair to stand on.

"Here, can you help Mommy break the end off?" she asked, handing her a couple green beans.

"I wants one like yours," Jade said, patting her on the arm.

"One what, girly?"

"One this." The toddler pointed to Kiera's apron.

"Oh!" Kiera giggled. "Hang on while Mommy gets you something."

The best thing she could find was a dish towel to tuck into Jade's collar, but she made a mental note to sew a tiny apron for her daughter's third birthday.

"See. Break them like this and put the icky parts in here," Kiera explained the delicate process of preparing green beans.

Jade threw hers into the bowl. "Plop!" she mimicked.

"Plop!" Kiera put hers in the bowl.

"Plop, plop, plop," Jade turned the silly word into a little song. Then she stopped suddenly. "That

Daddy?"

Kiera listened to the tires on the driveway and moved to look out the window. "That's Daddy. Let's surprise him."

She picked up Jade, and they hid around the corner to the front door. "When you see him, say 'boo'!" Kiera whispered.

Jade stayed impossibly still, sucking her thumb.

Brennan opened the door, and they sprang out from around the corner. "Boo!"

He jumped and they all shared a good laugh. Kiera handed Jade to him.

"Hey, what's this?" he asked, playing with Jade's dish towel apron.

"I gots one."

Brennan looked at Kiera for clarification.

"She was helping with dinner and wanted an apron," Kiera explained.

"I dill the laundwy!" Jade's eyes got big for emphasis.

"Really, can you show me?" Brennan asked. He set Jade down and let her lead him to the kitchen.

Kiera grinned as she listened to their conversation while she set the table.

"Are you going to tell me why you are grinning like a fool?" Brennan spoke from behind her.

"Oh, I was just enjoying the toddler conversation," she said, trying to swallow her smile as she carried the lasagna to the table.

"Jade tells me she talked to Uncle 'Torn' today. How is he doing?" Brennan leaned against the counter.

"He seems to be doing all right. Encouraged, at least." She twirled her ring, watching it glow in the light of the dining room. "And he said I could tell you that he and Jessica are in a courtship."

Brennan gave a slow smile. "You've been waiting for that, haven't you?"

"Am I really so obvious?" She grinned.

"You and Destiny, two rotten peas in a pod," he said, eyes sparkling with held-in laughter. "And now…" he let his hands rest on her shoulders, "I have some exciting news for you. My visit to Thorne got approved."

Kiera covered her mouth in delight. "Oh, Brennan, that's wonderful! I'm so happy for you."

"I checked the huge packet of paperwork they sent, and I'm allowed to take one adult with me. And being eighteen does count." He smiled with one corner of his mouth.

"You mean…?" She stopped short, and he nodded.

"Your mom offered to babysit Jade, if you'd like to come along."

Kiera shielded her face with both hands. "I can't believe it! I'd love to."

"Well, then. Let's get packing."

"You be good for Grandma and Grandpa, okay?" Kiera kissed the top of Jade's head. "We'll be back soon."

Jade turned to Brennan and bounced on his hip. "Daddy, is you going too?"

"Yep, Princess." He pulled her into a hug, and she wrapped her baby arms around his neck.

"Thanks so much for offering to watch her, Mom." Kiera hugged Mom and sent a loving look over her shoulder at the toddler. "You'll help her call us every day, right?"

"I will, sweetie."

A hug for Daddy next.

"You two have a good time, Sparrow," Dad said, untangling his hand from her hair.

"I will. And I'll be sure to tell you both everything about Thorne." She folded her hands. "I only wish you were coming with us."

"It's okay." Dad put his arm around Mom, and they brought out their brave faces. "We'll get approved soon."

"I'll be praying you are." Brennan set Jade down and shook hands with him. "We better get going if we want to arrive before dinner."

Kiera nodded and pulled her coat back on, then followed Brennan out the door. On the sidewalk, she turned for one last wave just in time to see Jade blow a kiss. She smiled and blew one back, then opened the car door and got in.

Brennan turned on the heater, and the windows grew foggy as the car shifted into traffic. "I'm glad I could get a half day of work today. We'd be getting there at midnight."

Kiera smiled. "How many hours driving is it again?"

He glanced at the screen. "Estimated four, but we'll see with traffic."

She nodded and rubbed her window clear with her sleeve. Four hours of conversation. She hadn't thought of that detail when she'd agreed to go. Kiera paged through her mental list of conversation starters and stared out at the traffic. The cars zipped by in shades as various as Jade's coloring supplies. Large video displays along the road alternated between fiery war images and perky newscasters.

She glanced at Brennan, suddenly realizing she still hadn't spoken to him. He hummed under his breath, tapping the steering wheel with his fingers.

"What song is that?"

"Hmm?" He blinked, seeming surprised to see her there.

"You were humming something. I just realized I've never heard your music before, and it sounded interesting." Kiera shrugged.

"Okay. Yeah." Brennan was sorting her words in his mind. "It's a song about God's pursuing love. I can play it for you, if you'd like."

"Sure!" She tucked her legs up in her seat and leaned against it, turning slightly toward him.

With a twitch of his fingers on the car screen, the first notes sang through the speakers. Kiera listened to the words, surprised by the simplicity but depth she found there. The jubilant rhythm turned the shifting of the cars outside into a dance. She looked at Brennan, and the thought she discovered on Easter came back again. He was comfortable with her.

Conversation was only awkward because she searched for something important to say. Friends didn't do that. Friends let their thoughts become words without trying to change them.

"I love it." Kiera's voice was low with awe when the song had finally faded away.

Brennan looked at her, smiles in the corners of his eyes. "Show me one of yours."

"Okay." She turned away slowly to her purse, hesitant to break the smile between them. "Have you heard 'Sparrows', the original version by Jason Gray?"

"I think so?" Brennan squinted. The car changed lanes.

"Well, I should warn you, I can get a little excited when it comes on." She pulled up the song on her device and turned on the wireless connection.

Brennan fiddled with the car screen. "Looking for it… Hang on… Spycraft4? Is that you?"

Kiera laughed. "I'm using the old family device. Ian named it. He's always had a spy thing."

"Gotcha. And we're connected."

The notes of her sparrow song shone into existence, and she felt the joy well up inside of her. So many memories connected to each line. Humming broke out of her thoughts, and she heard a light drumming beside her.

"Remember it?" She grinned at Brennan as he entered into the spirit of the song.

"Now I do!"

Kiera sang along and drummed on her knees, rocking back and forth in her chair.

Brennan used the steering wheel, dashboard, and side door as a drum set. Kiera laughed to herself as she watched him. If only Destiny could see him now! "Serious" indeed! This was more fun than she had ever had with him. More fun even than dancing around the kitchen with Kent. She sobered at the thought of him but let it slide away as the last chorus came on.

"Wow." Kiera caught her breath as the song ended. "You must have been a terror back when you had that clunky manual."

Brennan grinned. "Let's just say everyone around me is a lot safer now with this self-driving system. Although, I did drum a little less then. I had to use my elbows to steer."

"Okay, not funny," Kiera scolded, but the smile didn't leave her face.

"Don't worry. It was never when Jade was with me."

"I feel slightly better."

He just smiled, shook his head, and chose another song off the display. They were listening to an obscure soundtrack from a movie she'd never seen when the traffic slowed.

"It's exactly four," Kiera announced, checking the device.

Brennan grinned and shook his head. "Happens every day, almost right on the minute. I could get home half an hour earlier if it weren't for this."

"Hey, but at least it's epic," she joked as the song swelled and grew in volume. She sat up straight and made a noble face. Shading her eyes with her hand, she asked, "Do I look anything like that warrior princess?"

Brennan squinted his eyes and looked at her sideways. She felt suddenly shy under his scrutiny but forced herself to keep a straight face.

"You look more like a Lewis and Clark painting or something." He raised his voice over the music.

Kiera snorted and broke character. His eyes were sparkling at her, and she knew he was joking.

"Besides," he turned away as the car shifted into a gap in the next lane over, "that warrior princess dies, so…"

Kiera crossed her arms. "I'm still not sure I believe you. If it's true, that's a horrible spoiler. But would you give away something that big?"

He winked, and she caught her breath. Such a Thorne thing to do. A moment later, he laughed.

"What is it?"

"The car's trying to tell me our speed, and its calculation's in the decimals. Look."

Kiera leaned over to look at it, and a grin stole across her face. "I should send Destiny a picture. She'd get a kick out of that."

Brennan leaned back so she could reach across and take a picture with her device.

"All right, now look at me and prove you're not as serious as Destiny thought." Kiera held up the device.

Brennan let his face droop into a frown, holding back a smile.

She giggled.

"You're not morphing me to look like a kitten or something, are you?"

"I hadn't thought of it, but now that you mention it…" Kiera smirked wickedly.

He grabbed for the device, and she jerked her hand away from him.

"You'll ruin my reputation with her. I must stay Ogre Brennan, or she will make me adopt more kittens."

Kiera could barely understand what he said through her own giggles.

"I shouldn't have loaned you my books. Now you're as frightening as that warrior princess."

"Yes, but does she actually die?"

"I'll never tell."

"Then you shall become a kitten."

The car lurched forward as it sped up.

"But what if Destiny makes us adopt more kittens? Do you really need more to keep track of?" The car slowed down again.

"All right, I won't. Call it pax?" She stuck out her hand.

Brennan shook it and smiled. He checked the time. "We're definitely going to be getting there late for dinner."

"Oh, that reminds me!" Kiera slid the device into her purse. "I accidentally made us trail mix. This would probably be a good time to get it." She unclicked her seat belt and turned around in her seat.

"Accidentally?"

"It was supposed to be cookies." Her answer was muffled as she smashed her face against the side of his seat and rummaged in the ice chest on the back seat. She returned to her seat a moment later and put the jar of crumbly trail mix in the cup holder. Brushing her hair back from her face, she strapped back in and explained, "I tried a new cookie recipe, but they wouldn't stay together. I added dried fruit and chocolate chips. Tastes pretty good."

Brennan took a small handful. "Yeah, not bad."

The jar was empty and a blue and gold city night was falling around them by the time the car parked at their hotel. A sea of cars and lanes stood between them and the arched door to the lobby.

Brennan unstrapped and ran his fingers through

his hair. "It's a little bit of a walk, and this doesn't seem like a safe neighborhood. We should stick together."

Kiera nodded and pulled on her coat. He opened his door and stepped out into the empty parking space. She slid out after him before he could shut his door.

Two rolling suitcases and an ice chest. The wheels of the suitcases clicked along on smooth pavement behind them. Kiera glanced up at the glittering windows of the hotel and pressed closer to Brennan as raucous laughter broke out behind them.

His free hand closed around hers.

CHAPTER TWENTY
Paperwork

Kiera yawned and sat up. Her hotel bed had been ridiculously comfortable, but between the night noises of the city and her wandering thoughts, sleep had stayed just out of reach. She squeezed her thumb.

The device chirped, and she fumbled for it. A text from Brennan.

> Breakfast on the way? The sooner we get to the office, the less we have to wait in line.

She voice-texted back.

> I just woke up, so give me a few, and I'll meet you in the hall.

Time to move. Pajamas swapped for skirt and shirt. Socks onto feet. Feet into boots. Where was her hairbrush? She gave her hair the last few strokes as she stepped into the living half of her suite. Her makeup bag and mirror rested on the counter, and she stooped down in front of it to apply a quick swipe of mascara. Makeup didn't help much when her eyes felt like raisins, but maybe she'd be more awake later.

Another chirp from the device. She pulled it from her hip pocket.

In the hall.

Kiera: Coming.

She ran the brush through her hair again and pinned a strand back from her face.

She opened the door to see Brennan leaning against the wall with his arms crossed. He greeted her with a tired smile. "Good morning."

"Hi." Kiera twisted her ring and fell into step with him.

He spoke again when they were on the elevator. "You sleep okay?"

"Not really." She shrugged.

"Me either."

The morning air was cold on their faces as they walked to the car. Brennan touched the door handle, and the car unlocked. It was a short drive to the city jail, but long enough for Kiera to get a glimpse of the massive buildings and fractured humanity that lined the streets.

Her thoughts turned to Thorne as they waited in line. He lived in this sanitized but worn building, day after day. Inmates with stories as wicked as the devil surrounded him behind bulletproof glass walls. Guards paced up and down the halls with stun guns and scowling faces.

Kiera shivered and rubbed her upper arms. He shouldn't have to be there. He hadn't done anything wrong. The line moved forward, and she glanced at Brennan. He didn't look any more rested than she felt, and he nervously raked his fingers back and forth through his hair.

"Next," a worn official intoned, and they were standing before the desk.

"I'm Brennan Stewart, and I was approved last week to visit someone here." Brennan shoved his hands into the pockets of his khakis to keep them still.

The official typed something into the device wordlessly. Her blunt bob fell forward to cover her face. She grunted a moment later. "Okay. And who is this with you?"

"This is my wife, Kiera. I was told I could bring another adult with me." Brennan turned to her with a small smile.

"Full legal name, date of birth, national registration number." The official's eyes bored into Kiera.

Kiera stepped forward slightly and recited the information needed.

The official's fingers slid back and forth across the screen. "Just recently turned eighteen."

It wasn't a question, but Kiera nodded anyway.

"What is your status with the armed forces?"

"Um," she looked at Brennan, wondering what this had to do with anything, "I'm exempt."

"Religious or medical?" The official took two small devices off the shelf next to her and turned them on. So this was just small talk.

"My county has an exemption for mothers. We don't have enough funding for childcare."

The official raised one eyebrow but recovered herself quickly. "You'll need to put proof of residency in the paperwork as well. No felons are allowed to visit the inmates, even if the offense is just draft dodging."

She slid the devices toward them and gave a rehearsed speech. "Here are your devices. Mrs. Stewart, this one is yours. You will have significantly more paperwork to do. Your responses will be recorded wirelessly in our secure server. You are welcome to stay in the lobby or leave the premises. Please be advised there is a federal fine for damage to the devices or falsification of information."

Brennan thanked her, and they turned away.

"You good?"

Kiera felt him looking at her. She caught her breath and gave him a small smile. "Yeah, I just don't like interrogations."

"I know a place around here that serves clean food. Let's grab lunch and work on these there." He gestured toward the devices.

"I'd like that."

She found words again when they were seated in a corner booth at a little sandwich shop. The rich smells of baking bread, grilling meat, and fresh vegetables filled the room. Setting the device on the table, she leaned her elbows on the edge and looked around. "Have you been here before?"

Brennan took a sip of water. "All the time when I was in college. It was one of the closest places I could find that didn't serve radiation."

"What do you recommend?" Her mind tried to imagine him in college. A little younger, a little more relaxed maybe. Definitely a crazier driver.

"I always get the cold cut sandwich and a milkshake." He grinned sheepishly. "Basic but good."

"Sounds amazing."

They programmed their orders into the device fixed to the table, and the food arrived soon after. Kiera pulled up the first page of questions and took a long sip of her milkshake. It was as good as Brennan had said. The questions were basic name, number, and address ones until page six.

"Do these questions strike you as a little invasive? I mean, they already know all of this, I'm sure," Kiera said, filling out the names of her closest family members. Brennan and Jade counted, she realized.

Brennan scooted closer to look over her shoulder. "It's probably just a mini lie detector test."

She looked at his screen. In the place of parents, he had four names total. "Did your grandparents adopt you?"

"Yeah, Shannon and I both." His voice was quiet.

"What was she like? Shannon, I mean. I think Jade looks a lot like you, but some days I think I see her parents I'll never meet." Kiera wished she could take the words back the moment she said them, but it was too late.

Brennan avoided her gaze, instead pulling his device out of his pocket and scrolling through it. He swallowed, and Kiera turned away. She shouldn't have asked.

"This is Shannon. It's the last picture I have of her." Brennan's voice brought her thoughts back to him.

A blonde young woman with a thin face and shining blue eyes stared at her from the screen. Her hair fell in rich waves around her shoulders. A mischievous twinkle in her eyes reminded Kiera of Jade immediately.

"She's beautiful, and I can tell she was your sister."

He slid the device back into his pocket. "They adopted us when I was twelve and she was ten. I could have made it happen sooner, but I was afraid." Brennan studied his hands.

Without thinking, Kiera slipped her arm around his neck and waited for his next words.

"Dad was a nice enough man usually, but when he drank, the smallest thing made him angry. He and Mom used to fight, not just with words, and when that happened, I always took Shannon upstairs and made her stay under her bed until it was over. I didn't want him to ever touch her." He reached up absently and stroked the tips of Kiera's fingers on his shoulder. "One day, though, I don't know what got into me, but I got between him and Mom."

His voice caught, and Kiera tightened her arm around him.

"I started vomiting at school the next day, and when I complained of vision issues, they knew I had a concussion. The social workers were at our house within hours, and Shannon and I spent the night at G-mom's."

Kiera blinked back the tears that were rolling down her cheeks and whispered, "I am so sorry."

Brennan gave a little sad smile and ran his finger across the device screen. "It's in the past now. On dark days I still wonder if I had intervened earlier," he shrugged, "told someone, maybe called the police one of those times, if Shannon would have turned out differently."

"What do you mean?"

"All those times underneath her bed, and that last fight—she saw it, Kiera, she said I went flying—all those times, she grew bitter from them. I had no Gospel to give her, and later when G-mom and Grandy tried to share it with her, she wasn't open." His eyes were heavy, and she knew his heart was too.

"I'm sorry." Kiera felt ill at the pain she never

could have guessed. "I don't know what to say."

"Thank you for being here for Jade. It's all up to her and God, of course, but I pray every day her story will end up differently." Brennan reached out to her free hand and felt her ring with the tip of his finger.

"Her life already is so different. You've been a big part of that." She smiled up at him, trying to let him see the hope his bravery brought to her.

"Thank you, Kiera." He looked at her for a long moment, then let his gaze shift to the devices. "We should get this finished up. The office closes in a few hours."

"Right." Kiera slipped her arm from around his neck, and they scooted apart again, but she knew that somehow they would always feel closer now that he had told her his worst memories and deepest fear.

Kiera bit deep into her sandwich, savoring the flavors. Soon their lunch dwindled to crumbs, and they signed their names and fingerprints on the devices. They were last in line at the jail office.

A new official wordlessly took their devices, wiped them, and brought up the information on the main device before her. "I'm just running this against the database, but it looks like you have everything in order. Would you prefer electronic or paper passes?"

Brennan and Kiera exchanged glances.

"We'll take paper, please," Brennan decided.

Streets choked with traffic lay between them and the hotel, and Kiera sank into her seat, clutching both passes in one hand and Brennan's fingers in the other. Tomorrow she would see her brother.

CHAPTER TWENTY-ONE
Heightened Security

Kiera rocked on her heels and looked down the long line stretching before them. Apparently, this office handled more than just jail visitation. The line moved slower than the traffic she and Brennan had been stuck in. She shifted impatiently and gave Brennan a nervous smile when she saw his eyes on her.

"Only seven more people to go," Kiera said, reaching into her purse to make sure the pass was still there.

"Yeah." Brennan crossed his arms and stared at the line as if willing it to move more quickly.

"Next please," the voice of the official from the day before broke into the room, and they suddenly realized they were standing before the desk.

Kiera fumbled in her purse for the pass, and Brennan pulled his from his pocket, smoothing out the bent corners.

"Kiera Stewart, Brennan Stewart. You're visiting

together, right? Adults under twenty-one must be accompanied by another adult." The official didn't show any recognition of them. Her eyes and voice were hard, and her short, straight hair did nothing to soften her features.

"Yes, we're together," Brennan answered.

"Let me just process these passes, and then you'll be walked through the scanners," the official said, taking their passes to the back room.

Kiera felt tired enough to lean her elbows on the counter, but she couldn't help but wonder how clean it was. Another official appeared moments later, his features tight and eyes penetrating.

"We're sorry for the inconvenience, but there seems to be an issue with your passes."

Kiera darted a quick glance at Brennan and felt her stomach drop. This couldn't be good.

"If you could please make your way to the chairs over there," he gestured, "we'll send someone to talk to you soon. We're investigating the problem, and everything should be resolved very soon."

They found themselves ushered toward the chairs before either could speak, and the official was gone within moments. Kiera put her elbow on the arm of the chair and leaned her head against her hand. A yawn and a prayer coursed through her. She could see the officials through small slits between the blinds, and they rushed back and forth like ants, answering calls and scrolling through gigantic devices.

"What do you think is wrong?" Kiera asked, turning toward Brennan.

"I'm not sure," he answered, but his face told her he had a guess.

Their official strode out of the office and held out a smile to soften her words. "The security level of your passes is not high enough for the inmate you are visiting. They will need to be upgraded. Fortunately, you have most of the information already in place, but we'll need to interview you more extensively before it can be decided if you are allowed to visit the inmates."

Two security guards shuffled out behind her. "They will show you where the interview rooms are. If you would please leave all devices and personal items with me, we'll return those to you after the interviews. This shouldn't take very long."

Kiera handed over her purse, and Brennan gave them his device and wallet. She pushed closer to him as they watched the official put them in a locker.

"What's going on?" she whispered, unable to raise her voice from the questions that tightened around her stomach.

He shook his head and gave her hand a quick squeeze. The guards showed them down the hallway to two small rooms equipped with screens and cameras.

"Your interviews will be conducted via face call. If you need anything, just knock, and we'll be happy to help you."

Kiera sat in the rolling chair and heard the door click shut behind her. "Lord, please help this to be a good thing. An easy one. I'm not sure I can bear waiting any longer to see him."

A face blipped up onto the screen and a voice came through the speakers. "Hello, I'm Annetie, and I'll be your interviewer today. You've already filled out the basics for your low security level pass, but I have just a few quick questions for you. This won't take long."

The "Annetie" smiled, and Kiera felt herself relax slightly.

"First one, your maiden name is Clark. How long ago did you get married?"

Kiera looked down at her ring. "Just a few months ago, actually. Right after my birthday."

"I see. Just when you became eligible for the draft."

Kiera's stomach tightened.

The interviewer nodded and marked something on a device offscreen. "The inmate you are visiting also uses the last name Clark. Are you related to him in any way?"

"I'm his younger sister."

"I see. That must be really hard on you to have him in jail. I'm sure you miss him a lot."

"I do." Kiera's voice dropped, and a tear threatened to slip down her cheek.

"How often did you see him before?"

"Sometimes he would come over during the week, but mostly it was just on Sundays, during church."

The conversation continued, questions about church, questions about her family, questions about her friends. No questions about Brennan or Jade.

"Thank you for your time, Kiera. I hope they get you processed soon."

The device shut off, and Kiera stood up and knocked on the door. The guard opened it, and she and Brennan went back down the hall to the same chairs with the same official.

"Thank you for answering our questions; here are your things. We will record this information, and you'll receive word on your status tomorrow morning."

"Tomorrow morning?" Brennan's voice was even, but questioning. "I need to get back for work. Is there any way this could happen faster?"

"I'm afraid not. It's highly irregular for anyone to be allowed to visit an inmate in such a high security area, so the process may take a while. I'm very sorry. I hope you enjoy your stay in the city and get to see your brother and friend soon."

They were on the streetside before either of them spoke again.

"That was really weird." Kiera stepped back as Brennan opened the car door for her.

He got in the car as well, and both doors sealed shut. "Jessica and Pastor Silas visited him just over a week ago. I wonder if they had these problems too."

Kiera turned away and pressed her palm against the fogged window, feeling the coolness through the glass. The city blurred before her eyes as her tears mingled with prayers. She would have to be patient just a while longer.

"I can get another day off work," Brennan announced over a dinner they only picked at. "Do you think your parents will be okay with watching Jade an extra day?"

Kiera nodded. "I'm pretty sure, but I'll ask." A few taps on her device and an answer appeared. "They're happy to. Also, they're praying."

Brennan nodded and swallowed.

"Do you think it's too late to face call with Jade?" Kiera asked, pushing her plate away.

"Yeah, I think we'd better get back to the hotel. We can call her first thing in the morning." Brennan stood up and paid for their meal.

The lobby of the hotel was empty except for a forlorn luggage rack and the night receptionist playing matching cards on her device. Elevator doors glided shut behind Kiera and Brennan, then opened again when they reached their floor. Kiera held her device up to the lock of her room, and the door swung open. She stepped back to let Brennan through first and waited just outside the door.

He walked around the room, checking the windows, the closet, and the bathroom. "Looks like you're good." He passed her again and stood in the hall, leaning in the doorway.

"Thanks for checking. It's goofy, but it makes me feel much better." She entered the room and set her purse down on the kitchenette counter.

"No problem. And if you need anything, call me. I'll be in the car." His hand slid down the doorframe, and he turned to leave.

"Wait, I thought you'd be just next door. Like last night and the night before." Kiera felt panic slowly rising. Their car was three floors and a sea of other vehicles away. "You're gonna sleep in the car?"

"I'll be okay. I'll run the heater if it gets cold." Brennan swiped his fingers through his hair. "I only budgeted for two nights of hotel rooms."

Kiera twined her fingers together and her words spilled out over each other. "I can sleep in the car, if you need. I don't sleep well in this room anyway. I hear too many night sounds and last night I thought someone was hacking the lock to my door. I kept the lights on and hid in the bathroom until I was sure they were gone."

"Why didn't you tell me before?" Brennan's face scrunched in concern.

"I was gonna call you if something was actually wrong, but I'm probably just jumpy." She looked down. "I've only been gone from home overnight once, and that time Dad slept against the door." Kiera buried her hands in her hair and shook her head. When she looked up at Brennan, there were faint tears in her eyes, and she broke into an impulsive smile. "I'm sorry."

Brennan looked at her for a long moment. "Would...would it make you feel better if I slept against the door?"

"Yeah, I think it would." Kiera twisted her ring.

"Okay, if you're sure."

She nodded.

"I'll check out and get my stuff. You'll be fine?"

Kiera nodded again and shut the door behind him. Taking the comforter and an extra pillow off her bed, she put them on the floor by the door and rummaged in the ice chest for a snack. Dinner had been the last thing on her mind, but now she was too hungry to ignore it. Moments later, she heard a knock on the suite door followed by a message from Brennan, announcing it was him, and she let him in.

"I randomly got hungry." She gestured with her apple to explain it.

He rolled his suitcase into the kitchen and sat down on the counter. "Do you have something I could eat?"

Kiera handed him an apple and leaned against the counter next to him. Her mind tried to turn to worries and questions, but she forced herself to taste the apple. Listen to the air conditioning. Her apple shrank away to a core, and she threw it in the trash can.

Kiera turned to Brennan. "I left some extra bedding by the door for you. Thank you for doing this."

"It's really no problem. I'll probably be more comfortable there than in the car." He smiled a little.

"Well, goodnight then." Kiera retreated toward the door of the bedroom.

"Goodnight, Kiera."

Kiera was cold in her room without the comforter, but she wrapped the sheet tightly around herself and soon fell into a deep sleep.

The harsh notification of a device broke Kiera's sleep. She rolled over and groaned.

Brennan's voice carried from the other room. "Kiera, I think that's yours."

She pulled herself out of bed and stood up. What time was it? The device blared again, and she murmured, "I'll get it. Hang on."

Draping her sheet over her shoulders like a shawl, she smoothed the wrinkles out of yesterday's skirt and stumbled into the kitchen.

"Hello, this is—"

"Hey, Sparrow." Ian's voice interrupted her. "I have something really important I need to talk to you about. And your husband too if he's available."

"Okay…" Kiera paused to register his words and blink herself awake. "Brennan, he wants to talk to you too."

She heard him untangle from his blanket and come

to stand behind her.

"Something's happened, and I think you should come home right away."

Kiera covered her heart with her hand. "Is Jade okay?"

"She's fine as far as I know. It has to do with who you are visiting, and why you've been unable to. If you go home now, we'll bring Jade to you and explain more."

Brennan's hands tightened on Kiera's shoulders. "I was wondering. We'll start out right now."

"Good. Turn off all devices and drive manual if you can."

"Will do. Thank you, Ia—"

"See you all later." The voice call ended.

Kiera stared at the device as she powered it down. It wasn't just a function of slow government. Something was actually wrong. Their visit wasn't happening. Hot tears filled her eyes.

She could feel Brennan's hands on her shoulders. Tracing comforting circles on them. Trying to ease the tension and fill her with peace. But the unsettled feeling in her stomach wouldn't go away.

"It's about Thorne, isn't it?" Kiera asked her brother point blank as she sank back into the couch. She squeezed both thumbs so hard her nails bit into her palms. Jade stretched in her sleep and her feet dangled off Brennan's lap onto Kiera's.

"In a way, but it's actually more about you." Ian thumbed his chin. Rachel stood behind his chair, her face solemn but gentle.

"I know I've always been a bit of the family conspiracy theorist, but after what happened today, I think it's time to step up security. That's why I had you stay off devices on the way over. I'll try to get you modified ones soon, if I can."

"What are you talking about?" Brennan stiffened.

Ian looked from one to the other.

"It wouldn't be on the news yet," Rachel said quietly, resting one hand on her husband's shoulder and the other on her protruding stomach.

Ian sighed. He looked so worn he could have been the oldest brother. "They are changing Thorne's crime from civil rights infringement to...well, using an old term...treason. Since I work in the foreign office, they put two and nothing together to get four and a story. Apparently, Thorne 'sold secrets' to the Russians."

Kiera shook her head and rolled her eyes. "They're just making things up now. That'll never hold up in a court of law."

"They can make it if they want to," Ian answered. "And more. They are watching all of us and our second cousin's neighbor closely at this point, so once again we need to be careful." He leaned forward. "Be careful. No need for more Clarks to get picked up."

She nodded and her hands shook. She would

follow his device instructions. "What does this mean for Thorne? And for you, since you work in government?"

"Thorne will be undergoing another trial, and frankly I'd expect a harsher sentence. The lawyer team is on it, but we can only hope," he said, trying to sound comforting. "I, on the other hand, am not in trouble yet; but I do need to lay low. Rachel too, since she worked in the department for a few years. We'd like to leave town for a few days when the trial end time is scheduled. Things could get a little wild. Do you think you all would be willing to take care of the kids?"

"Anything to help," Brennan offered, and Kiera quickly agreed.

"Then pray for all of us and stay off those devices," Ian said, rising to leave.

They let him and Rachel go without another word. Kiera covered her mouth with both hands and sobbed. In one swift move they had changed it from a religious matter to a political one. Where would Thorne find support now? What did a harsher sentence mean?

Brennan laid Jade against her shoulder, and she wrapped her arms around her daughter.

"C'mon, let's pray." He began to pray aloud, and Kiera's crying grew quieter.

CHAPTER TWENTY-TWO
Babysitting

Kiera jolted awake and sucked in a breath. Wrapping her blanket tightly around herself, she clutched at the edges. It was only a dream. But why did a dream have to be so close to the truth? Only two days until the verdict, and her nieces and nephews were coming tomorrow. It was finally real.

She flopped back down on her pillow, nearly hitting her head on the headboard, and stared at the ceiling. Tears rolled down her cheeks and into her ears as the scenes of her nightmare replayed in her mind. Each dream was the same; they always took Thorne away to a place he could never come back from. This time they had gone one step further and given him life termination.

"Lord, he'll just get life imprisonment, won't he? My imagination runs away into horrible places. I should be worried about having the kids here. I should be wondering how Thorne can marry Jessica if he's in jail forever. I should be worried about church. I shouldn't borrow trouble from something that likely will never happen."

She scooted down into her blankets and pulled them up around her. A spotlight of early morning sunshine penetrated through the curtains. "But that's what worries me, Lord." She was whispering now like she didn't want to admit the next words. "I know capital punishment hasn't happened since Mom was a kid, but they have surprised us before. Like with pulling that 'selling secrets' trick. Just, please help me be ready for whatever happens."

She lay still for a long moment and yawned, but her eyes refused to close with every inch the sun climbed higher in the sky. Muffled sounds came from the kitchen, and she smiled as she realized Brennan was already up. He got up with the sun, why couldn't she? She threw back her blankets and hurried to change into everyday clothes. Maybe having someone to talk to and starting on her to-do list longer than both arms would keep the nightmares away.

She threw on her favorite skirt and shirt combination and ran a brush through her hair. A quick glance in the mirror showed circles forming under her eyes and a worry not even makeup would hide. She sighed and brushed her hair back from her forehead. Time to face the day.

The smell of brewing coffee hit her right away as she entered the kitchen and a very wide-awake

Brennan turned to her. "You're up early. Good morning." He wore a faded work T-shirt, and a hard hat sat on the kitchen counter.

She managed a sleepy half smile and found a tea bag before he could offer her coffee. "Sleeping was not gonna happen, and I thought I could get started on some things anyway since the kids are coming tomorrow."

"Sorry I won't be here during the day to help, but I'll pitch in like crazy in the evenings." He cracked an egg into the frying pan and reached for a fork.

She handed him one. "It's okay. I figure if I plan meals, naptimes, and activities, it should work." She hesitated, then asked the question on her mind. "Do you think it would be all right if we use our devices to watch the verdict? Everyone's going to be watching anyway, so it's not like they will be able to pinpoint us exactly."

"I don't know. You could ask Ian when he gets here. Sound good?"

She nodded. Carrying her mug of hot tea over to the table, she leaned her chin on her hands and stared sleepily out the sliding glass door. If only her thoughts would collect themselves well enough for her to write a to-do list.

"I usually do my devotions about now. Since you're up, would you like to join me?" Brennan asked, setting down his breakfast.

"Oh. Sure. Yeah, I'd love that. I left my Bible

upstairs though." She moved to stand up.

"It's okay. We can share." He scooted his chair closer to hers and flipped open his Bible to the middle of Matthew.

She realized sometime later that he had been reading and she had let herself fall into staring out the window again. She had always thought of herself as a morning person, but apparently not *this* early. Drawing her thoughts back to the present, she began to listen.

"'Now brother will deliver up brother to death, and a father his child; and children will rise up against parents and cause them to be put to death.'"

She shivered. "Or church members, in Thorne's case."

"But look what He says later in the passage." Brennan pointed to a verse.

She read aloud. "'And do not fear those who kill the body but cannot kill the soul.'" Her stomach clenched. "'But rather fear Him who is able to destroy both soul and body in hell. Are not two sparrows sold for a copper coin? And not one of them falls to the ground apart from your Father's will. But the very hairs of your head are all numbered. Do not fear therefore; you are of more value than many sparrows.'"

"He's got it all covered. He knows what's going on," Brennan said quietly around a mouth full of food.

"I know." Kiera squeezed her thumb under the table. "I just hate that the sparrows still fall, you know?"

He nodded and looked down at the table.

"But I keep reminding myself that, whatever happens, He is still good."

They shared a smile, and Brennan stood up, laying a hand on her shoulder. "I have to get going now, but I'll be praying for you today."

"Thanks," she replied, watching him go. "Can we do this again tomorrow?"

He paused in the doorway, hard hat in hand, and his face seemed to light up. "We can if you like."

She twisted her ring for a few moments before standing up and grabbing a piece of scrap paper and one of Jade's crayons. She had a list to make before her little sunshine woke up. The tape over the camera and speakers of her device reminded her not to open it, and she settled for humming her favorite song about sparrows.

Kiera dried a dish and stood on tiptoe to put it in the cabinet. She yawned again, but being a little sleepy was worth having time for devotions. She felt bolstered and ready for the day, and Brennan had made her promise to text if she needed anything.

Ian and Rachel would arrive within the hour, and she hurried to have the kitchen sparkling before the doorbell rang. She opened the door and took her sleepy nephew from Rachel. Two little girls squirted past them, chattering excitedly about the pink backpacks they carried, causing Rachel to laugh merrily as she set the diaper bag on the kitchen table.

"How are you, Kiera?" she asked with a hug.

"I'm okay." Kiera managed a smile. "Nervous, but okay."

"Thank you so much for doing this. I don't know how we can ever repay you," her sister-in-law said.

Ian and their oldest boy shuffled through the door with various bags and stacks of bedding.

"No need. I like borrowing my nieces and nephews," Kiera answered, giving her brother a side hug as Rachel began to explain the luggage.

"I brought bedding for everyone, and they each have a bag of clothes for today and tomorrow."

"And breakfast," Robbie added toothlessly, rhythmically tapping on the cooler.

Rachel put a hand to her baby bump and caught her breath, turning to Ian. "Is that everything?"

He nodded and gave her a reassuring smile. "Kiera, I had a friend modify devices for you and Brennan. They should be safe to use for anything, though you will find a few features, like face calls, missing. We were also able to retrieve most of your files." He held out a device. "This one's yours."

"Thank you." She smiled a little when she realized he had matched it to her old one as best he could. "What is this one codenamed?"

"LittleBlueNest. Everything about it made me

think of you. Of course, Brennan's is Superman, and that's mostly a joke." He winked in a way that made her ache for Thorne and remember her question.

"Can we watch the trial verdict?"

Ian and Rachel exchanged glances.

"It's safe to…yes."

Kiera nodded. It probably wasn't the best idea, but she didn't want to find out the sentence secondhand.

After enough conversation for Baron to grow heavy in her arms, Ian and Rachel left her with five children and the rest of her day.

"Robbie, please carry the sleeping bags up to the loft," she directed, laying the toddler on the couch. "Audrey, I'll need you to set the table, and—"

"What do I do?" Sophia asked, tugging on her arm. Her dimpled face was framed by tight brown curls.

Kiera smiled down at her niece and thought for a moment. "I need you to take all of the bags and set them near the couch. I'm going upstairs to get Jade. Can you all be done before I get back?"

The encouraging sound of "yes, ma'am" followed her up the stairs.

"Hey, girly!"

Jade struggled to stand up and gave her a sleepy smile. "I eats breakfast?" She rubbed her eyes and reached out.

Kiera scooped her up in a hug. "Yes, in a minute. Did you know your cousins are here?" She switched out the toddler's sleeper for an everyday dress and continued to talk as she tamed curls into pigtails at lightning speed. "There is Robbie, and Audrey, and Sophia, and then Baron, who is almost as tall as you are."

Jade yawned. "We play dollies?"

"Yes, you'll probably play dollies." She brought Jade downstairs and was immediately greeted by the sound of crying.

Audrey was doing her best to hold Baron, and Sophia stood nearby looking worried. Robbie tried to explain over the loud crying. "He was looking for Mommy, and Sophia told him that she wasn't here."

"But then I told him she was coming back," Sophia was quick to explain.

"And then he fell off the couch," Robbie added, hands in the pockets of his grass-stained jeans.

Kiera took him from Audrey and put him on the hip opposite Jade. The day was beginning to look very long. Hopefully breakfast would fix a few problems.

"All right, everyone. To your chairs!" she commanded cheerfully.

There was a mad scramble. She graduated Jade to a big girl chair and put Baron in the highchair. His tears quickly dried when she set out the homemade granola bars, applesauce, and turkey slices Rachel had packed.

"Daddy usually prays at breakfast," Sophia said in her little voice.

"Robbie, would you be willing to pray for us?"

Kiera asked.

He nodded solemnly, and she bit back a smile as he directed everyone to hold hands while he prayed. "Dear Jesus, thank you for this food. Please help Daddy and Mommy to have a good time together, and help Aunt Kiera not to be worried. Amen."

Kiera opened her eyes and blinked back the tears. How had he known?

Audrey taught Jade to remove the chocolate chips from her granola bar and set them aside "for dessert" while Robbie bit a smiley face into his turkey and showed it to everyone who would admire it.

"That's a very nice face," Kiera said, the third time he showed it to her. She reached to give Baron more applesauce.

Sophia bit off a bite of granola bar and asked, "So are you the Mommy?"

"Yes, I'm Jade's mommy." She smiled and passed Robbie another piece of turkey.

"Our mommy says that we are staying at your house like when we went camping," Audrey added, tossing a few of her dessert chocolate chips into her mouth.

Jade copied her.

"Can we have a tent?" Robbie asked.

"Right after breakfast," Aunt Kiera promised.

Robbie shoved the rest of his turkey into his mouth, and the others rushed to finish their food as well. Audrey was so eager to clear the table that she got an angry slap from Baron, who didn't think five servings of applesauce was enough. Kiera stepped in quickly, and soon the girls were findings socks and shoes while she and Robbie did the "heavy work" of carrying chairs out into the backyard.

Kiera's new device chimed in her pocket, and she stopped on the porch to check it. It was from Brennan's work device.

After that roadtrip, it feels weird to go somewhere without you.

She grinned to herself and sent a smiley face that matched her expression. That was an "I miss you" if ever she'd seen one. She texted back before she could stop herself.

I miss you too.

CHAPTER TWENTY-THREE
Shadow Puppets

The backyard was full of happy shouts and running feet. Baron and Jade chased each other in giggling circles while Robbie and his sisters debated remodeling the tent. Everyone had woken up with extra energy after their naps, and Kiera hurried to prepare dinner so she could get in on the fun and supervise a little more closely.

The screen door opened and Robbie entered. He shoved his hands into his pockets and asked, "What's for dinner?"

She smiled at his eagerness. "I'm making sandwiches—do you want to help?"

He tapped thoughtfully on a loaf of almond bread that had been set out to thaw. "Do you have something interesting I can do?"

"Would you like to slice the cheese?" She set the cheese slicer on a plate and handed him a block of cheddar cheese.

He was humming happily when the screen door opened again, and Audrey struggled Baron into the house. "Aunt Kiera, he's stinky, but he wouldn't go in when I told him to," she explained, brown ponytail falling over one shoulder.

She set him down, and he collapsed to the ground, shooting out a trembling lip in defiance. Jade watched wide-eyed and sucked her thumb while Sophia pushed past them to investigate dinner. Kiera picked him up under one arm just as another crisis began.

"Robbie! What happened? Did you let Sophia use the cheese slicer?!" She set Baron down and jerked the slicer away, setting it far back on another counter. Prying Sophia's hand open, she examined the girl's finger. The cut wasn't deep, but it was bleeding a lot, and she grabbed a rag to wipe it clean before bandaging it. Sophia whimpered and tried to move away.

"Sophia, hold still. It'll be all better in a minute," Kiera soothed.

The doorbell rang, and Audrey ran to answer it.

"Don't answer it! If it's Daddy, he'll let himself in. Just...nobody move for a second!"

Audrey retreated to a corner and hid behind a picture book, and the other children fell silent. Moments later, the tension eased as Brennan let himself in, and Jade ran to hug him. The others crowded around, chattering about tents and sandwiches, and pulled him out the back door before he could get a word in edgewise. Kiera excused herself to finally change Baron.

She shook her head when she realized how she had treated Robbie. And Audrey. She had no right to take out her worry on them and would have to apologize as soon as possible. Tickling her tubby nephew, she giggled along with him and stood him up from his diaper change.

Excited conversation met her from the kitchen, and she entered to find everyone seated in their chairs, munching on sandwiches. Brennan sat at the head of the table, holding three conversations at once and passing out food. He was such a Godsend! Something in her face must have betrayed her thoughts because he smiled shyly and ran his fingers through his hair.

Kiera slid Baron into the highchair and took the empty seat next to Robbie. "Hey, Rob. I'm sorry I was angry with you about the cheese slicer. Will you forgive me?" she whispered.

He grinned and nodded.

She was getting lessons in biting her bread into a spaceship shape when Jade yawned.

Brennan ruffled her curls. "Don't fall asleep yet, Princess. The evening's not quite over."

"I not sleepy, Daddy."

Audrey sat up on her heels. "What are we going to do, Uncle Brennan?"

Sophia's face echoed her question, and Kiera and Robbie paused. The toddler in the highchair just kept ripping his cheese into tiny pieces and hiding it in the cup holder on his highchair tray.

"Well..." Brennan paused for dramatic effect. "I was thinking if we helped Aunt Kiera with the dinner chores, we could play shadow puppets in Jade's room. Is that good with you, Kiera?"

"Sure!"

Brennan and Audrey carried teetering stacks of plates to the kitchen, while Robbie filled the sink with soap and a little water. Kiera opted to leave Baron in his cheesy highchair and tied dish towel aprons onto Sophia and Jade.

"We are gonna get done so fast!" Sophia declared, her cheeks dimpling.

"Yes, you're right." Kiera smiled at her niece and her daughter. "We're a good team."

When the last dish was dried and the table clean, Brennan announced, "All right, troops, everyone ready for bed, then gather in Jade's room."

The nieces and nephews stampeded up the stairs, with Jade following as best she could.

Kiera had two sleepy toddlers cuddled up in their cribs by the time the others were ready for bed. There was much discussion and rearranging before Brennan arrived with a flashlight. His eyes traveled to the second crib, and he jerked visibly when he saw Baron.

Kiera looked away and squeezed her thumb in her apron pocket. Maybe she should have asked him if Baron could use it. She ventured another glance at him when he was showing Sophia how to make a rabbit in front of the flashlight beam. She could almost imagine traces of tears in his eyes.

"Ooo, Daddy, is that a bunny?" Jade took her thumb out of her mouth and pointed.

"Yep, her name is Carrots," Sophia explained, making her rabbit hop up and down. "She's happy because her birthday is tomorrow. Audrey's turn!" She slid off Uncle Brennan's lap.

Audrey chose a butterfly and hummed a little tune as she made it fly gracefully back and forth. Robbie found this exceedingly boring and immediately asked to learn a crocodile when it was his turn. Sophia made a puppy, and Audrey flew her butterfly around again, this time landing on a flower Aunt Kiera helpfully made. Uncle Brennan flew a bee into the scene, and a hilarious debate about who could fly faster had everyone in giggles.

Kiera's flower shook with laughter.

"Oh, dear! Is that an earthquake?" asked the bee.

Sophia giggled.

"Ah, no! It's a crocodile!" The butterfly flew away, leaving the bee and the flower to be eaten in one gulp.

"Guess we know who could fly faster," the crocodile said in a deep, silly voice, earning more giggles.

They made more puppets until Jade and Baron fell asleep, Sophia was blinking to stay awake, and it was officially time to say goodnight.

When her nieces were tucked into their sleeping bags, Kiera slid into bed and turned out her lamp. She sighed happily. It had been a good day. Maybe tomorrow would be too.

Kiera shielded her flashlight as she snuck past Robbie into the kitchen. A handful of chocolate chips sounded particularly good now that she had remembered what tomorrow was.

She bumped into a device sitting on the counter, and the screen displayed a webpage right when she realized it belonged to Brennan. Why did she recognize the site name? She shook the question away.

There were much more important things to worry about, and among them, she couldn't find her chocolate.

CHAPTER TWENTY-FOUR
The Trial

Kiera opened the device and willed her stomach to settle. Live footage of the trial streamed on mute, but so far it was all preliminary legal jargon.

Kiera smiled slightly as the camera moved to her brother. His hair and the shadows under his eyes were grayer. He sat, patiently and peacefully, ready to answer any question they gave him—if only they would.

She gritted her teeth and squeezed her thumb. From the few thin facts laced with hyperbole she could decipher, she knew they had done a good job sewing their story up tightly and branding him "Hitler of the year".

"Aunt Kiera." Sophia patted her arm over and over. "Is the cookie dough ready now?"

She turned to look at her little niece and the three other children sitting patiently at the table with cookie cutters and rolling pins ready. Her heart warmed and she slid the news app to the side. "Yes! I think it is. Should we listen to some music?"

Sophia clapped her hands and danced in place. She pushed her head under Kiera's arm and helped choose a song. Together they retrieved the frosty bowl of sugar cookie dough. Kiera set it down in the middle of the table and grinned at her crew. "Ready to roll?"

Cheers erupted and little hands reached out for their portions. She handed a ball to Robbie and to Audrey, then showed them how to roll it out. Giving a smaller piece to Sophia, she tried to help her form it into cookies but soon decided it was best to let her be. The ragged dough would soon be inedible, but at least she was having fun.

"All right, Jade," she said, sitting down in a chair next to her daughter. She swiftly rolled out a slab of dough and helped her press the cookie cutters into it.

Jade grinned up at her. "We's making alllll the cookies."

"Aunt Kiera, I'm making this one for Daddy," Audrey interrupted, pointing to the man-shaped cookie on her cutting board. She rocked back and forth on her knees in the chair.

"That's very nice, Audrey."

"I'm making this one for Mommy!" Sophia piped up and smashed her dough into one big ball again.

"And I'm making one for everybody. Is Baron too little to have one?" Robbie asked.

"No, he can have one," she assured him.

Jade patted her arm to get her attention. "I hash one too?"

She grinned and nodded. "Hey, do you guys know this song?"

"Mommy plays it!" Audrey exclaimed, lifting her eyebrows in excitement. She touched one of her braids, coloring the strands white with flour.

Kiera's "sparrow song" started into the chorus, and they hummed along. She let the words and the joy of the little ones touch her troubled thoughts.

"Daddy?" Jade asked, perking up at the sound of the garage door.

Brennan let himself in, and she ran to hug him, then pulled him over to the table. "Daddy, we makin' the cookies."

"Nice, Princess. I like your horse, Robbie," he said, inspecting them and smiling in a tired way.

"See mine?" Sophia asked, and Audrey interrupted to show off a butterfly.

Brennan brushed past Kiera's chair and whispered, "The trial?"

"Nothing conclusive yet."

"Aunt Kiera, my pan is full."

"Mine too."

"Well, then it's time to put them in the oven." She smiled at the children and stepped into the kitchen with a pan in each hand. The music had stopped, and she gave in to the temptation of checking the trial footage.

Something was different. She knew it immediately. Setting the cookie sheets on the counter nearby, she refreshed the page and stared at the screen in horror.

"'For the First Time in 20 Years: Thorne Clark to Receive Highest Form of Punishment'." She mouthed the words, but no sound would come out. Touched the screen with a shaking finger. Opened the article with a barely audible whimper. Official government news, not some fake clickbait story. Did this mean what she thought it did?

"The Federal Court of the United States has tried and found former pastor Thorne Clark guilty of hate speech and high treason against our land. In the recent objective against Russia, important defense secrets were leaked, causing a high loss of American and UN life. Justice demands the highest form of punishment—effective termination of life—to stop this threat and tell Russia they will not infiltrate us again."

The words "effective termination" blurred in front of her and she fell to her knees, covering her face with her hands. Sobs rose in her throat, choking her and wracking her whole body with an aching sorrow. She let out a small scream.

"Mommy, what's matter?" Jade said, pulling at her hands to try to see her face.

"Get Daddy, just get Daddy," Kiera whispered, red-faced and tear-drenched. This could not be happening! She needed someone to wake her up from this dream.

"Kiera?"

She staggered to her feet and pointed to the screen. "Tell me, Brennan. Is this real?"

He read the words and grew rigid.

"Brennan, don't you know what this means?" She felt like shaking him, or sobbing into his shoulder, or slapping him. Anything to get him to speak. She needed him right now, and all he would do was stare at the wall. "Brennan?"

He looked at her and his eyes were dull. Somewhere else. He raked his fingers slowly through his hair but stopped halfway and let his arm drop. "Two in a row. I don't know what to say. I—I think I should go upstairs."

Tears drowned her vision and she shook her head. Not now, please. Then she would be alone. But he didn't stay. He melted out of her cloudy vision upstairs behind a closed door.

"Oh, Lord, help me, please." She was shaking now. Like a leaf being torn from a tree.

"Aunt Kiera?" Robbie hesitated in the doorway, eyes large, and she beckoned to him.

He and Jade and Audrey and Sophia wrapped their little arms around her. Living and breathing, whole humans. She could hear their heartbeats pulsing in rhythm.

"Aunt Kiera, what happened?" Audrey's voice was next to her ear.

Kiera released the children and looked at them for a long moment. "Uncle Thorne... Uncle Thorne is with Jesus."

Jade's eyes brightened. "Oh, he likes Jesus!"

"You're right, Princess. You're right."

Kiera wandered around the living room, scooping up toys and letting them slip out of her arms again. Her nieces and nephews were gone, picked up that morning by their grieving parents. Jade was taking an indeterminately long nap, and Brennan hadn't left his room.

Tears gathered in her eyes at the thought of him. She hadn't realized just how much she valued him until he was gone as well. But more than that, she wanted to know how he was. Her hesitant message had not been answered, and the thought of him crying alone in his room was one she couldn't think long without crying again.

She lay down on the couch and let the stray tears darken the cushion under her cheek. She was so tired. Tired in body. Tired in emotions. Tired in her soul. Her brother was gone. Just with the prick of a needle. She hadn't even been able to say goodbye.

The realization hit her again, leaving her limp and angry. She turned her face into the couch to muffle her sobs and punched the pillow over and over. The government had needed a scapegoat for a lost objective and chosen the first person available—a pastor who stood for what he believed. Her brother.

The device chirped at her. She ignored it. The outside world breaking into her day always meant no good. Though maybe if someone was contacting her, she at least wouldn't be alone. She stumbled across the room like a seasick passenger, holding her pounding head.

A message from Jessica showed on the screen.

Kiera, I have something for you from Thorne. I'm dropping by to give it to you. I think it's important.

She thought of answering Jessica but all her words were broken. Jade called from upstairs, giving her an even better excuse. She brushed her frazzled hair back from her face and tucked it behind her ears. Putting on her best "happy mommy face", she climbed the stairs and lifted Jade from her crib.

Dinner was apples and crackers for Jade since she was the only one in the house who felt like eating. Brennan never showed up to try. Kiera was still sitting in front of her plate, absently watching Jade dress dolls in the living room, when the doorbell rang. Jessica.

The young woman's eyes were rimmed with traces of smeared mascara, and the smile she gave was sympathetic and tired. "How are you doing, dear?" she asked quietly, hugging Kiera.

Her simple, kind question broke the dam of tears

Kiera had been holding back.

"Oh, Jessica! I still can't believe this happened! What is God doing?"

"I don't know, Kiera, I honestly don't know yet. But I think the letter I have for you might help." Jessica kept her arm around the younger woman's shoulders and led her to the couch where she handed her a folded piece of paper.

"When did he give it to you?" Kiera asked, fingering the paper.

It was Jessica's turn to tear up. "I didn't get to see him that last day either. Neither did Papa. We tried, but—" She broke off and when she spoke again her voice came out in a pained squeak. "The pastor that spoke to Thorne right before he went to Jesus happens to be a friend of Papa's and made sure we got them."

"Oh, I'm sorry, Jessica! I assumed..." Kiera hugged her friend.

"It's okay. I should go home now and be with Papa, but do you want to pray with me?"

Kiera wiped her eyes and sniffed when Jessica was gone. She had been crying for two days already, but the sweet, short prayer had still been able to make her cry again. She picked up her letter off the couch next to her and tucked the one marked for Brennan into her pocket. Then she slid off the couch and sat down with her back against it, legs crossed.

Dear Kiera.

She looked up from reading and smiled. She could almost imagine him winking as he wrote it.

I get to be a martyr. I just found out today, and to tell the truth, I'm excited. Don't think me perfect—I didn't like the idea originally—but God and I have been talking, and I'm good with it now. I know you will be all right, little sister, if you remember how much He loves you and works things for good. Hug Jade for me. I love you very much.
Until later,
Thorne

She held the letter to herself and rocked back and forth, crying silently.

CHAPTER TWENTY-FIVE
Brennan

Jade was in bed, and the house was quiet. Kiera dragged herself up the stairs, heart aching and chocolate chip stash empty. She paused in the loft and twisted her ring. Brennan's closed door seemed like a stone wall between them.

She should knock. See if he wanted any of the dinner, breakfast, lunch, and another dinner he had missed. See if he wanted to pray together. Maybe read that passage in Matthew again.

Her dry tears came out in a little sob, and she covered her mouth with a shaking hand. But he didn't want her. She knew that. She was only here because of Jade.

Kiera turned toward her room, but the rustle of paper in her pocket stopped her. Thorne's letter. For Brennan. She strode across the loft and slid it under the door, then sank down and leaned her head against the cool wood between them.

CHAPTER TWENTY-SIX
Rain

Kiera stared at the unfamiliar ceiling. Why was she lying on the nursery floor again? Then she remembered. She didn't want to be alone. Unclenching her sore fingers from the leg of Jade's crib, she sat up and rubbed them awake. A shard of early morning light tumbled in through the curtain, but it shouldn't have. Nothing should have been the same, but it was. Everything was normal—almost everything.

She smoothed her limp hair back from her face, leaned against the other crib, and let her eyes travel to the peacefully sleeping heap of Jade. She had hugged the little girl so many times for her brother since Jessica brought her his note. The tears came to her eyes, and she choked back a sob hiding her face on her drawn-up knees. Why, God? Why?

She felt like screaming again. Standing up quickly, she left the nursery and sought refuge in her closet. Tracing her fingers along the texture of the wall, a new question came to her. What was she doing so far from home? There was no one to talk to except herself. It would be so easy to leave. She could have the car drive her to Mom and Dad's and send it back within a few hours.

The tears came to her eyes faster and harder as she gathered up her belongings and threw them into a box. She tore clothes off their hangers, wadded them up, and shoved them in. Books piled in after. She tossed the one belonging to Brennan onto her bed. Her extra shoes flew in, along with the crafting supplies she had planned to decorate her room with.

That was everything, right? Everything except the "treasures" in her windowsill. Picking up the shells, she dusted them off and wrapped them in a stray sweater. Now for her bird's nest. She cradled it in her hands and remembered the night she'd found it. A curled piece of paper was nestled into the edge.

Kiera set the nest down and opened the paper. She knew these words. She didn't want to read them, but something made her. "Love is not [merely] affectionate feeling but a steady wish for the loved person's ultimate good as far as it can be obtained."

She crumpled it up and threw it across her room where it fell just in front of the door. Hiding her face in her hands, she said aloud, "Why do You keep bringing this quote back to me? It doesn't mean anything. Not now."

The tears in her eyes swallowed up her vision like

raindrops on a window. She sank to the floor, the silence wearing heavily on her. God didn't care about how much she was hurting. Didn't answer her questions. Didn't send someone to hold her. The anger filled her, sapping away her energy and making her ribs ache.

Kiera laid her cheek against the carpet and looked at the fibers, lined up like little rows of grain. She smoothed her fingers across it, watching the color change between light and dark. What was she doing doubting God? She was as small in His eyes as the fibers she touched. Small in the universe, and small in His plans. He didn't have to care about her.

Shuddering sobs shook through her, but the sound of them seemed to come from far away. She reached up for the nest and pulled it close. The twigs cut into her arm, but she held onto it all the same. The birds that had lived there were known by their Maker.

"Hold me, please, like one of Your birds. I want to trust that Your goodness and Your love are enough. I really do." Kiera sat up and folded her knees close to herself. Tears constricted her face, pulling at her forehead. "Show me, please."

She laid her forehead against her knees and muffled her sobs in the skirt of her nightgown. Her shoulders relaxed with a shudder, and a peace settled around her like a blanket. Kiera worked a tangle out of her hair with trembling fingers and glanced toward the overflowing box blocking her closet door. What had she been doing?

She rose to her feet and slowly walked toward it. "I was gonna leave. Give up. But You never do that, do You? Love gives, even with nothing in return."

Tears streamed down her face as she realized the hard decision before her. It would be lonely. It would be hard. But she would love Brennan and keep her commitment to stay. She began to hang her clothes in the closet again. Books back on the shelf. Shoes in their place. Crafting supplies neatly stacked.

Later when everything was back in place, Kiera crawled into bed with the quote clenched in one hand. One more prayer fluttered in her mind. "Be with Brennan, please."

She fell asleep, resting in the knowledge her prayers would be answered.

Kiera buttoned her black coat with one hand and dragged her umbrella in the other. The weather app had promised rain later in the day, but she prayed it would hold off a little. This day would be hard enough without radiation nausea added. Jade caught hold of her hand, startling her. Neither she nor Brennan had thought to guide the little girl to the truck.

Glancing at Brennan, she picked Jade up, opened the side door, and strapped her into her carseat with as bright a smile as she could manage. Inside she felt like a smashed piggy bank held together only by rubber bands and thinly spread glue. The metaphor would have made her smile if it hadn't been the awful truth. Kiera moved to climb into the back seat with Jade, then squeezed her thumb in her pocket and felt the thin piece of paper.

She sat down in the passenger's seat instead.

"Is this the address?" It was the first time Brennan had spoken to her in days.

Kiera nodded. "They couldn't find a church that would rent to us, so it's all at the gravesite."

He didn't answer as he programmed the address into the vehicle. She leaned against the window and stared out at the picture-perfect houses. Jade hummed happily in the back seat, and the umbrella fell down into the footwell. Kiera wasn't sure what to pray for; she had prayed so much and cried so much in the last few days that she felt empty.

As the truck accelerated onto the freeway, she ventured a glance at Brennan. His hands were tight on the wheel and his eyes stared dully straight ahead. Though he didn't show it, she knew his thoughts and emotions were swirling by the way his recently combed hair was stirred. She hadn't thought of it before, but didn't he say once Thorne was one of his only friends? Her eyes began to cloud with tears, and she turned away again, this time to pray for him.

The truck stopped in the parking lot of the graveyard, and the wind whipped at her coat as she got out. The unwanted rain would be coming soon.

Grabbing Jade, she followed Brennan to the pavilion where her family was already standing.

Mom and Dad hugged her tight, and she cried into them for a long moment before finding a place in the circle. She registered the faces of her brothers and their families, stooped Pastor Silas, haggard Jessica, and Aric looking much out of place and uncomfortable with his own tears. Destiny stood just behind him and telegraphed her sympathy across the pavilion.

More vehicles drove into the parking lot. Church people coming to pay their respects. They spoke to various members of the Clark family in quiet, sorrowful tones before finding places to stand near enough to hear what was happening. The cars continued to come into the parking lot with somber-looking people swarming out of them until there were vehicles parked along the street edge, and still more came.

Aric bit his lip. "Better not be a riot," he muttered in a low tone, but Kiera heard him. Had there been riots?

Everyone waited in tense silence as the newcomers shuffled into place. With Jessica's help and a cane in one hand, Pastor Silas moved to the front and looked at the crowd with a sad, sweet smile. "Could the pallbearers please come forward?"

Kiera sucked in her breath and covered her mouth with her hand as her brothers and dad moved toward the hearse. Deacon Tiegler and Deacon White followed them respectfully, and Brennan extricated himself from the crowd to join them. They carried the casket toward the center of the pavilion and set it on a stand.

Kiera was shaking now with silent tears, and she clung to Jade as Brennan returned to his place next to her. Pastor Silas prayed, and they sang a hymn—Thorne's favorite. He used to sing it while he was scrubbing the dishes. Ian had joined in before she and Jordan ran through the room with pots and pans as "percussion".

Pastor Silas was reading now, Scripture probably. She looked across the way at Aric. He had that same look of deep concentration on his face as when he used to drink in Thorne's sermons. This was Thorne's last sermon—his coffin was proof that God meant more to him than what any man said, and he was willing to go to his Father. A smile lit Kiera's face for a moment as she pictured him grinning with Jesus over this testimony.

Mom and Dad were standing up front now. She choked, and Niyanna put an arm around her. Mom had a piece of paper in her hands, and she was trying to read it.

Kiera remembered another time she had looked this way. Thorne had written her a letter saying he wanted to be a pastor, and she had cried for joy. Only this time, the tears weren't happy ones. Mom shook her head and handed Dad the paper to read.

He began to read in a quavering, broken voice, and Kiera knew immediately that it *was* the very same letter. Words like "calling" and "testimony" and "evangelism" spun around her ears, broken apart, but she knew what they meant. Family member after family member and even several church members went up to speak and to cry, but her feet were rooted to the spot. Even Brennan went up to say something. Waiting until the last moment, she dragged herself to the front with Jade on her hip.

She waited until her voice was steady and twisted her ring as her eyes focused on a tree far at the edge of the field. Dropping her gaze, she looked at the crowd, not registering faces, only the number of them.

"My name is Kiera Stewart, and I am Pastor Thorne Clark's sister. If he could be here with us today, I think he would thank you all for coming to support him and his testimony for the Lord. He also wrote me a letter last week the day before he went to be with Jesus."

Her voice broke, and her eyes found Brennan. He was crying, and somewhere underneath those tears his eyes were bluer than she could have imagined. Her heart ached and went out to him.

"He told me that I needed to remember two things. God loves me, and He will work everything out for good. Now, I don't know what the good is yet, but I've asked God to show me and I trust Him to. But I do see His love in you all coming out today to support us. To prove that Thorne Clark didn't die as a criminal, but as a martyr. So thank you."

She was done speaking, and the pallbearers were carrying the casket away. Someone handed her facial tissue to wipe her tears and nose, and she was enveloped in hugs by several women she failed to recognize. Each family member put a shovelful of dirt on his casket. Kiera's hand shook as she helped Jade. The tractor and the landscapers would do the rest.

The rain started to come down in needle-like drops as the crowd dispersed. Kiera followed her family to the parking lot where they exchanged hugs and memories all around. Strapping Jade into her carseat, she stopped and stared at Aric and Destiny getting into her parents' car.

Rachel noticed her looking and explained, "No one in their family would give them a ride, so your parents offered. Aric might stay with them awhile too, since things are pretty stormy at home with Kent leaving."

A shiver went up and down her spine as she registered what this meant. Her parents were still reaching beyond themselves, despite their grief, to serve the Lord. More good that had come from this.

The raindrops were falling faster now, and Kiera searched the parking lot for Brennan. He was still at the graveside. "Rachel, would you stay with Jade a moment?" She started across the grass without waiting for a reply.

"Brennan." She ran her hand down his coat sleeve and caught his fingers with her own.

He spoke, voice cracking with emotion, "My life has been full of people, good and bad, but Thorne was my first real friend." He stared out at the newly placed metal plaque.

Thorne Malachi Clark. 30 years old. A messenger of God. Kiera read the words again and felt drops of rain touch her forehead.

"He always sent me back to God with whatever problem I had—even in that letter he gave me." Brennan's voice was choked with tears, and Kiera felt her own wet cheeks. "I must have forgotten about it; I found it on my bedroom floor. When did you get yours?"

Kiera swallowed. "Um, Jessica delivered both of ours a few days ago." She smiled in a grimace. "I slipped yours under your door." She broke out into fresh tears at the memory of the painful loneliness. "I'm so glad you read it. I thought maybe…" She turned aside, then back to look up at him. "Well, you didn't message me back or come downstairs or anything, so I wasn't sure you could bring yourself to open it."

"Kiera." He turned to her, brow wrinkled and rain running down his face in little streams. "Please know I didn't stay away to hurt you, I just needed time to think."

She nodded bravely but knew, if she didn't leave now, she would break down completely. Disentangling her fingers from his, she moved away from him, but his whispered words stopped her.

"I didn't mean to hurt you, but I did, didn't I?" Pain washed across his face. "I'm sorry I shut you out, Kiera. He was my friend, but he was your brother." He looked down at her and closed his hand around hers. His words came barely above a whisper, "Call it pax?"

Kiera came closer again and lifted one corner of her mouth in a little smile. "Yes, and anyway, I'm the girl that hid in the closet, remember? Scared you half to death."

He returned her smile, like she had hoped.

She continued, words barely audible but from the heart. "But we're both here now, and if you want to talk or just stay silent, I'm your friend. I'm not going anywhere."

He put his arm around her and drew her so close there was no telling where his coat ended and hers began. She laid her head against him and felt his heartbeat echo deep inside her.

They chose the silence option. The rain fell in sheets.

CHAPTER TWENTY-SEVEN
Sparrows

Kiera stirred the spaghetti sauce and checked the long loaf of gold-brown bread warming in the oven. Her device chirped, and she moved to check it, being careful not to tangle with Jade and Flicker, who were crawling all over the kitchen floor on a grand adventure.

"Jade, Daddy's here!" she said, looking up from the message. "He's gonna park in the garage so we can help him carry in the groceries."

Jade sprang up and took her hand. "I is gonna help too?"

"Yep, you are a good helper to Daddy and Mommy," Kiera said, helping the toddler find her shoes. Slipping into her own mud-caked yardwork flip-flops, she led Jade out to the garage where the truck engine was powering down.

Brennan got out with a smile for both of them. The rolling garage door clicked shut, and Kiera let go of Jade's hand.

"What can I carry?" She held out both empty hands.

Brennan opened the side door and reached in, grabbing a bag full of lettuce heads. "I tried to get a variety, like you asked."

"Thank you. This looks great!" Kiera took the bag from him and lugged it into the kitchen.

"Ooo, Daddy! Strabewwies!" Jade hopped up and down, clapping her hands. "I eat all the strabewwies?"

"Later, Jade. But do you wanna help me carry them into the house?" Brennan took the small crate off the back seat.

"Um…yesh," Jade decided and reached out a hand to hold on to the crate.

Kiera followed them with a jar of milk and several cartons of eggs. "The cream on this is really thick. It'll be great for Jade's birthday ice cream," she told Brennan when the toddler was just out of earshot.

"That's good." He smiled at her.

Kiera filed the eggs into the refrigerator and spoke to Brennan again when he and Jade returned with the rest of the groceries. "Speaking of you-know-what, Mom has been asking if we have any gift preferences."

Brennan locked the door to the garage. "Just nothing noisy or electronic, but I'm sure she'll do great. She's pretty expert."

"Three boys in a row does make one a veteran," she answered with a smile that quickly faded as sadness threatened to overwhelm her.

Brennan reached for her hand and gave it a gentle squeeze. "Aw, come on. Weren't you noisy too?" he said quietly to gain a smile.

"Yeah, I had my moments. There was that one time I was playing Revolutionary War with Destiny, and we yelled 'the British are coming' so much we couldn't speak for a while after."

Brennan's blue eyes smiled down at her, bringing an answering one to her face. "Did she have a pitchfork?"

Kiera laughed and pulled away from him to stop Jade from eating a strawberry. "Daddy said wait, Jade."

Jade sighed and her very pigtails seemed to droop.

"Why don't you go find Flicker and see if she wants pets?" She bipped the little girl's nose.

"Otay!" Jade ran into the living room calling for her kitten.

"I better go change real quick, but I'll help with dinner when I get back. Deal?" Brennan said, setting the crate of strawberries up on the island.

"Sure thing," Kiera answered. She took the bread out of the oven and wrapped it in tinfoil and dishcloths, then tucked it into a basket. Next, she forked the squash noodles into a crock and was just pouring the sauce over them when Brennan returned.

"All right, what can I do?"

"I was just about to start hulling the strawberries, if you wanted to help." Kiera shrugged.

Brennan answered by grabbing a colander from the cabinet and filling it with several handfuls of strawberries. Kiera set out a cutting board and a paring knife but abandoned them moments later when Jade yelped from the living room.

"Princess, what's wrong?"

"The bad kitty jus' swat me," Jade pouted, flicking her hand in the kitten's direction.

Kiera knelt down, praying for patience. "Jade, did you touch the kitty's tail?"

"It was jus' waving at me." Jade shrugged, her whole face scrunched up.

"Flicker doesn't like it when you touch her tail. It's like if I pulled your hair. Flicker's tail is like her hair." She inspected the toddler's hand. Not even a scratch. "Don't touch Flicker's tail, okay?"

"Yes, Mommy. But she's bad!"

"She won't be bad again if you don't touch her tail." Kiera kissed Jade's curls and returned to the kitchen.

Brennan had already taken over her cutting board, and a pyramid of prepared strawberries sat on the edge.

"I can take that back now, if you want."

"No, it's okay. I like cooking, remember?" Brennan grinned. "Would you mind checking the weather? It looked good yesterday, but I wanna have umbrellas ready if we get rained out."

Kiera nodded and sat down at the dining table,

device in hand. The screen wouldn't turn on. "I think I ran it down by accident. Can I use yours?"

"Yes, it's on the counter." Brennan gestured with his knife.

She squeezed past him to the counter and traced her fingers across the scratched screen. The device was a different model than hers. Where was the weather app? Hopelessly buried in a bunch of complicated construction apps. She'd have to just use the general web app and hope it was easy to find there.

Sure enough, weather was the most frequently viewed page, but the one right after it made her pause. She glanced over her shoulder at him. Why did she remember this site name? She'd never been there before.

Kiera clicked the icon before she could stop herself. The app routed to the page for an adoption agency. An embryo adoption agency. The one Jessica had sent the link for in a conversation long ago. The page she had found open on his device the first time she had seen him cry.

Kiera's hands shook with knowledge as she scrolled down. *Fetus. Six days gestation. Preserved by carrier Shannon Stewart.* Her eyes blurred, but she could still see the words that followed. *Status: up for adoption.*

"The other crib," she whispered, heart aching inside of her.

"What's it looking like?" Brennan asked, and she clicked away quickly.

"Um, it's going to be perfectly sunny. It'll cool down in the evening, so Jade'll need a jacket if we're staying later." Kiera sniffed and wiped her eyes, then turned around.

A bowl. He would need a bowl for the strawberries. Too many on the cutting board. She reached up into the cabinet and grabbed a glass bowl, navigating it across the kitchen to him. Fumbled, but he caught it.

Blue eyes looking at her. "Kiera, are you okay?"

"What would you think..." She trailed off and twisted her ring. "What would you think of me adopting an embryo?"

He set down his knife and looked at her sideways, but she spoke again before he could.

"This is too much to ask, I know. I've already added to your expenses. But I feel I have to do this. The child has no chance. Jessica says they only have two years, and then they're aborted." She was weeping in desperation. "Brennan, I could get a side job. Sell something online. Do college. I'd pay you back—"

He took her hands. "I know. Two years, only. It's cruel." His voice shook a little. "Ever since I've known you, you've always cared about 'the least of these', but there's something more to this, isn't there?"

Kiera nodded, and he continued, "It can affect your own health and fertility. It often doesn't even work—I've read about it."

"But, Brennan, I—"

"I'm not saying no, I just want to know why."

"I know about Shannon's baby."

He dropped her hands, and everything in his face seemed to crumble. "It's dead. It's been two years. It's *dead*." He nodded as if convincing himself. "Two in a row. It and Thorne."

Kiera reached up to wipe the tears spilling down his cheeks and felt a smile all over. "No, it isn't. I just saw the entry!" She pulled him over to the device and explained as he opened the site, "There's a banner at the top apologizing that their site was down last week. Everything was being refiled or something to that effect."

He stared at the screen, mouth dropping open slightly. "Thank you, Lord, for giving it back to me," he breathed. He turned to her. "Thank you, Kiera."

Kiera grinned up at him. "So, can we adopt it?"

"I'm sure if you're sure." Brennan smiled slightly.

"I'm sure. But why didn't you tell me before?" They moved away from the device, and Brennan returned to the strawberries.

"I didn't want you to feel pressured. Like I was asking more of you than you've already given."

She looked down as the pieces began to come together. He had wanted her to have a choice—a real one. Her eyes traced his face, so full of love for God and his family. For her. It had always been there, she realized, barely contained, but she knew now that he had always been giving her a choice.

He felt her eyes on him and looked up. "What is it?"

"I love you. It's always been true, but I can say it now." She tried it on for size. "I love you, Brennan Stewart."

Brennan came forward, and his gentle fingers trailed down her hairline and behind her ear. He pulled her into a hug, and she buried her face in his shoulder, feeling his kiss on her forehead. "I love you too, my Kiera."

They were kissing almost before she knew it. Brennan's fingers in her hair, her arms around his neck in a hug. She could feel joy bursting inside like a sparrow in full flight. God had given her a good gift in this man.

Brennan's voice was husky next to her ear. "I have something for you, if you'll keep an eye on Jade and the strawberries for a moment."

Kiera let him go with a smile and watched him hurry upstairs. What more could he possibly have to give her?

"Mommy, we eats the strabewwies yet?" Jade wandered into the kitchen.

Kiera picked her up and leaned against the counter. "Not yet. They're almost ready, and then we'll go to Destiny's house and eat them."

"Does Deshiny have kitties?" Jade's eyes were big with hope.

Kiera laughed and hugged her. "I don't know,

Princess. But you will get to play a lot and see Grandma and Grandpa."

"And cows?" Jade clapped her hands.

Brennan entered the kitchen, hands behind his back. "Kiera, I… This is your engagement ring. I bought it with your wedding ring when I first knew I wanted to marry you—about a year ago. Long before the draft and Christmas even. I know we had to get married first because of the draft, but if you'd like to wear it…" He knelt down, the little box open in his hands.

Kiera reached out and ran her fingers through his hair. This man who had loved her for longer than she could have guessed, had loved her enough to wait. To let her choose to love him in return. "I would be honored."

She slid off her wedding ring, and he slipped the shining gold promise onto her finger. Then she replaced the wedding ring with its carving that looked like wheat. They fit together perfectly, and the stone of the engagement ring shone like a winking star. Brennan stood up and drew his arm around both her and Jade.

Jade pulled her thumb out of her mouth. "Now eat strabewwies?"

"Oh my goodness, dear! I thought you were never coming! Your dad has already practically won the baseball game. What took so long?" Destiny scolded. The skirt of her red paisley dress fluttered around cowgirl boots.

Kiera smiled as she handed Jade to her friend and shut the truck door. "Sorry, long conversation, but we're ready to party now."

"Brennan, what took so long?" Destiny bounced the toddler on her hip.

"Hello, Destiny. No pitchfork?" he teased, and she shook her head at him solemnly. "Where should I put this food?"

"Up at the house if it's cold, at the tables if it's not. Crockpots plug in at the porch," Destiny rattled off. "Kiera, there's someone you need to meet."

"Lead me there, I will follow," Kiera said, saluting her friend.

Jade giggled, and her hair bounced.

"Jade, I'm a fan of your hair. It's just another way you take after me." Destiny looked at Kiera and caught her hand. "Wow, you're wearing an engagement ring too?"

Kiera nodded, happiness showing in the color on her cheeks.

"You officially owe me a three-hour-long girls' only talk. I have an idea to disable your truck so you can stay longer if needed," Destiny said. "I snooped Aric's coding course. Some awesome things you can do to the self-driving mechanism." She cracked her knuckles.

"Oh, dear," Kiera laughed. "How are you all doing?"

"I heard from Dad a little last week, but he doesn't come around anymore." Destiny avoided her eyes. "Mom confuses me, and Aric seems to be doing well. You know your parents have been having him over once a week, right?"

Kiera nodded.

"I'm glad. It's good for him." Destiny smiled through her tears.

"But how are you, Tiny?" Kiera asked.

"I'm learning to love whatever God lets me have and hope in Him alone," her friend replied. "And, I discovered this recently, but it helps me—when Kent left he took his Bible."

"I'll never stop praying for him. We'll all pray for him," Kiera replied, giving her friend a side hug.

Destiny wiped her eyes. "But, anyway, enough about me. We're on a mission."

They walked over to the drink tables, and Destiny set Jade down. A young girl, as tall as Kiera, was leaning against the big tree that shaded the tables. Her eyes followed the baseball game until Destiny greeted her.

"Kiera just got here, if you want to meet her."

The girl turned and smiled. Her loose blonde braids brushed her shoulders, and thick bangs slanted across her face. Something about her struck Kiera as familiar.

The girl stuck out her hand. "I'm Mercy."

"Hello, Mercy. I'm Kiera."

"Kiera Stewart, right?"

Kiera smiled. "The one and only. And this is my daughter, Jade."

Jade waved and hid behind her legs.

Mercy leaned down and waved. "Hi, Jade."

"I call her my niece. She takes after me a lot, though I'm not shy." Destiny grinned.

"Do you know anyone else here, or should I play tour guide?" Kiera asked.

Mercy twisted her hands together. "We used to go to this church when it met in the building. When Pastor Clark was arrested, we stopped. Like a lot of other families did, I guess. But we went to the funeral two weeks ago, and God used it to remind us what's important. You can't give up on following Him just because it's hard; that's gaining the world and losing your soul."

"Oh, Mercy! That's wonderful! I'm so glad you all are back!" She hugged her new friend. "I've been asking God to show me the good in this, and I can't help but think this is an answer to my prayer." Her face broke into a smile that reached into every feature. "And I have no doubt He'll show me even more."

Mercy smiled. "Do you think they'd let us join the baseball game?"

"Of course they would! If my mom will watch Jade, I'll join you two in the outfield."

"Deal!" Destiny grabbed Mercy's arm, and the two raced off.

Kiera led her little girl over to a row of lawn chairs.

"Hey, Mom." She bent down to hug her. "Could Jade sit with you for a little bit? I've been invited to a baseball game."

"Sure," Mom said, lifting the little girl onto her lap.

"Thanks a ton." Kiera turned to leave. "Oh, and Mom, Brennan and I have a lot more to tell you. Can you all come over for dinner tomorrow?"

"I'll talk to Dad, but I think our schedule's clear. We'd love to talk with both of you." Mom's eyes smiled at her behind her glasses.

Kiera joined the girls far in the outfield, mostly away from the action but close enough to see the game. They were lining up to bat when Brennan joined her.

"I plugged in the crockpot and set the strawberries on the table." He wrapped his arms around her waist from behind.

"Thank you. You do realize you just got in line?" Kiera looked up at him.

"Think I can hit a home run?"

"I want to watch when you do."

She leaned into him and let the wind blow through her hair. Mercy had stepped up to bat, and Dad was coaching her, words gentle and advice sound. Kiera looked out over the field and saw in every face the love of God that was bigger than her understanding.

"Kiera, look!" Brennan's voice was just above her ear.

At the edge of the field, wings stirred into flight and a small flock of birds flew over the baseball game. Her breath caught in wonder. They were sparrows.

The End

The gangster slouched against the dumpster and drained a water bottle. Tapping his thigh impatiently, he peered down the alley as far as could be seen by flickering street light. A shadow appeared at the end of the street, and footsteps echoed through the lonely outpost.

He straightened and fingered his gun as the man drew closer. "Who's there?"

"You know who I am, Kent Moore, but don't bother saying it aloud. The cops would have a holiday if they knew I was here." The man thumbed his chin and took a step closer.

"What d'ya want?" he replied with an edge to his voice. One shot into the air was enough to call for backup, but for some reason he waited.

"If you ever want to quit serving the end of Arroyo's gun, let me know. I might have a job for you."

He drew his gun. "Git out of here before I use this."

"Fair enough." The man turned calmly and walked down the alley.

He slouched again, then stood up and yelled after him, "If I did want your job, how should I find you?"

The man turned to look at him but kept walking. "Don't worry. I'll find you."

Acknowledgments

This book you are holding in your hands would be nothing without the fabulous, supportive people who have helped me. I'd like to acknowledge and thank just a few of these precious real-life characters.

First of all, God Who laid this story on my heart and brought it together. There would be no book without You.

My parents who have been a great example of earthly love and my greatest encouragers. Thank you for the deep conversations and editing. Also, snacks for morale.

Perry Elisabeth, you are cool. I got a cool oldest sister. Thank you for the awesome cover design and interior formatting. I lurves it.

Aimee, thank you for listening to me jabber about this story for three years straight. :D

Paul, you've liked everything I've told you about this book, and that means much. Also, your further development of Ian in your book *Crossroads* helped me see him more clearly.

Anna, you're a goof-of-a-beta-reading-sister-crack-up-helpful-thingy. Fist bumps and firecrackers.

My younger sisters and my nephews, I love you dearly, you distracting inspirations. <3

The Awesome Mikayla, thank you for your enthusiasm, encouragement, beta-reading, and joyful emails. Jade and I both appreciate you.

Princess Kaitlyn, the popcorn war was for you. ;) You're a good friend to me.

Emily and two other sweet sisters from church, thank you for letting me test the entire plot of my story on you. Our conversations helped me know I might be onto something.

My Goodreads and Facebook communities, wow! Y'all are so good at naming kittens. XD

The Chatterbox Girls, this is the second project you've helped me finish. Y'all are the best.

My beta-readers for being such a fun, helpful crew! Angie, your help with consistency in word use and character points-of-view was amazing! Leona, thank you for the help with those stray commas. ;) Mikayla, see above. Angela Watts, thank you for catching those character details. Kellyn, the story has more clarity because of our conversations. Thank you all!

Kelsey Bryant, it was such a pleasure to work with you! You did an amazing job editing in the short time frame I gave you, and my book is much better because of it. Thank you so much!

If there's anyone else I'm forgetting, please know I appreciate you too. ;) Here's to more stories!

About the Author

Kate Willis hates writing bios but loves cheese. She has a pretty cool family who loves God number one, conversation second, and creativity third. A whole lotta awesome. She reads too much (mostly middle-grade fiction) but doesn't regret it. She's written some books, including this one.

Also By This Author…

THE TREASURE HUNT

"They were silent a moment each thinking of the strange clue and even stranger signature. Anna was first to speak. 'It seems like some sort of treasure hunt.'"

A boring summer vacation turns into an exciting adventure when Anna and her brother David discover a mysterious note. Soon they are hunting for clues, solving puzzles, and cracking codes—all on their own farm!

ENJOY THE POODLE SKIRT

"Rule one: Keep your hands clean.
Rule two: Careful with the food trays.
Rule three: Visit the soda fountain as often as you like, but don't make yourself sick.
Rule four: Enjoy the poodle skirt."

Canary is excited to spend a whole week helping her newlywed aunt and uncle run a 50s diner along with her older siblings Rose and Michael. Even the rules for working there are fun!

But when a routine cleanup presents a mysterious, hand-drawn map, her vacation gets even more exciting than a banana split with hot fudge sauce. And that's saying a lot!

A short story.

THE TWIN ARROWS

Two children. Two journeys. Twin arrows.

Ryla follows her father's parting instructions as closely as she carries his gift. Her protectors are kind, and safety is certain inside the convent's strong walls. But now she must leave and what lies ahead is uncertain...

Her brother Drewin won't wait any longer. The knight promised to escort him isn't coming, and gossiping neighbors threaten to reveal his identity. He strikes out on his own, sure he can outrun the danger...

RED BOOTS

"Old Joey's lips fell open in astonishment as he examined a pair of boots. They were bright red, standing out like a forgotten apple on an autumn tree. He whistled, long and low. 'Red boots!'"

A pair of shiny red boots bring unexpected Christmas joy to a shopkeeper and a little girl.

A very short story. (Approximately 8 minutes reading time.)

Made in the USA
Middletown, DE
17 June 2019